THE GUARDIANS OF STAGHILL

By the same author

THE HILLS ARE LONELY
THE RUNNING FOXES
THURSDAY'S CHILD
A CRY ON THE WIND

THE GUARDIANS
OF STAGHILL

Joyce Stranger

SOUVENIR PRESS

First published 1997 by Souvenir Press Ltd,
43 Great Russell Street, London WC1B 3PA
and simultaneously in Canada

ISBN 0 285 63361 9

Typeset by Rowland Phototypesetting Ltd,
Bury St Edmunds, Suffolk

Printed in Great Britain by
Creative Print & Design Group (Wales), Ebbw Vale

To Mark Viney, whose illustrations provide me with ideas for stories. *The Guardians of Staghill* was sparked by a picture of a fox in woodland, who becomes Ric in the story. Without that picture, this book would never have been written.

One

Torran was waiting. Usually the woods brought peace, and a release from care, but tonight she was uneasy. It had been a troublesome day. A rising wind sneaked through the trees. Branches creaked eerily. There were watchers observing her. She was as aware of them as she was of the ground beneath her feet and the stars in the sky above her, though she had no idea where they hid.

She was tempted to return home but she needed reassurance. If only he would come. She had not seen him for three days. He was her lifeline, her route back to sanity and security, and she needed him.

Eyes glittered in the moonlight, staring at her through the undergrowth. A lithe movement, a sudden bound, and the feral cat was gone, intent on hunting. Torran, startled, drew in a deep breath. Perhaps she imagined the observers.

Although it was so early in the year, there was a hint of spring. Far away a train raced through a tunnel, its horn blaring, the sound disturbing the night. Rustles and cracking sticks and small squeaks told of creatures searching in the undergrowth. A moment later came the long, slow call of a hunting owl, his mate answering.

She loved Staghill, which was so different from the brilliant tropical country in which she had grown up. It was a gentle landscape, a blending of soft shadows, under a calmer sun.

She and Jan Ardan, her step-grandfather, had lived in the cottage on the hill for eighteen months. The past was beginning, very slowly, to recede. The healing woods and

7

the wild animals that she met reached out to her, comforting her. Here she felt safe.

Tonight she needed that, but the feeling eluded her. She was afraid again. Two years ago to the day appalling events had marked her for ever. She now hated anniversaries. They brought memories that she would much rather forget.

She leaned against the twisted oak that spread its branches above the badger sett. The trunk was rough against her cheek. The sun was dying in a blaze of scarlet streaked with black clouds that forecast wind.

She had come to the woods early tonight, unable to bear the cottage. All day she and Jan had avoided the subject that dominated them. Every conversation seemed, inexorably, to lead in the wrong direction, so that both broke off in dismay. She could not paint; he could not find solace in the wooden animals that he carved.

Perhaps it would have been better to say, 'Do you remember?' and discuss what had happened, but that was beyond them both. They had never been able to talk about it, never been able to express the horror, or the misery, or even share the grief. The world they knew had ended that night, scarring both of them.

She turned her eyes away from the sunset. It reminded her of those other terrible fires.

The pool at the edge of the clearing was coloured. A red glow lit the covey of ducks and the two swans that glided regally on the water. They had flown in earlier that day, followed by a little skein of geese that called as they sped through the air. They had not landed.

The birds were tinged blood red.

She looked down. A beetle was crawling across the grass. It was very small, shining black, the wings and back edged with a brilliant blue. She was a monster in his world, an irrelevance. Would he even realise that she was alive?

Soon night would take away colour, but now she

watched its movements, wondering about it. Every blade of grass must seem enormous. Did he see the trees, or were they too big to contemplate? There at her feet was a whole universe, peopled by tiny creatures she could not even guess at.

She must ask Lyan Grant, the village schoolmaster. He came out sometimes at night to video the wild animals. He might know what kind of beetle this was. He had an uncanny understanding of the abundant life that shared the night-time woods. They had formed a fragile friendship, each respecting the other's need for privacy and solitude.

Tomorrow she would paint this scene: the dense bushes, the little glade and the ride that led to it from trees so overgrown it seemed impossible that even a mouse could penetrate them. She would paint the birds on the rippled water, and the willows that dipped their boughs as if to drink.

She was as much part of the night as the animals. She looked down at the village of Lynsom Green, sheltering beneath Staghill. The houses were dark blocks patched with light from uncurtained windows. Cars driving along the hilly streets sent their headlights upwards, scything across the sky. There were few street-lamps. They only lit the crossroads.

There was a glow in the church windows and the sound of distant singing reached her as the choir practised. The voices were balm, enhancing the peace that she felt here on the hill. An owl flew to a tree-stump a few yards away and perched there, his head swivelling. He did not see her. She was a deeper shadow against the dark tree trunk.

He had his nest in the barn in the farm below her. Last year he had reared three owlets. Soon there would be more to feed. He flew away on silent wings, the air hardly moving as he passed. Had he noticed her he would not have worried. He knew her, as she knew him.

9

The slim, brown-clad figure with its cap of dark hair and deep-set brown eyes in the heart-shaped face was familiar to the creatures that haunted the woods round the cottage. Her carefully chosen clothes helped to hide her among the dark trees.

In spite of the feelings that had overwhelmed her all day, excitement prickled, although she knew it might be followed by despair. It was time. He was late. He might not come at all. His behaviour was unpredictable. When he failed to appear she felt desolate.

The twilight faded. A full moon shone, dappling the ground. A small wind whispered, bringing the hint of returning winter and bitter cold. The sky was clear and there would be frost later. She looked up at the stars. There had been larger stars and a more brilliant night sky in the land where she had spent her childhood years, half a world away.

She seemed to have been waiting for hours. He must come. Tonight of all nights she needed him. Fear touched her, lest he had suffered some disaster.

One of the foxes crossed the clearing, turning to scent the air as it caught her scent. It might be Blacktip. She could not see his tail. He turned his head, one paw raised, looking straight at her, ears moving slightly to catch every trace of sound. In the distance another fox barked sharply, and he faded into the undergrowth and was gone. His mate was calling.

The badger sett beside her was deserted, but there was one in use on the other side of the pool. Four nights before she had heard the sounds of scratching and deep grunting, though as yet she had not seen the occupants. Lyan had captured them on video and promised to show her.

A shadow moved on the opposite bank: he was coming. She was almost afraid to breathe lest he saw her and changed his mind. He was the wrong side of the wind and would not scent her. She had taught him to be wary of all but her. If he thought a stranger stood there he would be gone.

Moonlight shone on the white coat, on the lifted head, ears fanning for sound. He had been enchanting when he was first brought to her.

He was now a magnificent stag, although his antlers had never grown. Others like him were known. They were called hummels, Lyan said. Perhaps the horn had never formed because of the lack of pigment in his coat. Perhaps, too, the energy that would have gone into their making had, instead, contributed to his size. He was bigger than any other stag on the hill.

He was not albino. His eyes were dark. Torran watched him approach, every movement cautious, asking the wind for news, listening for an alien footstep, ready to run and hide at the least hint of danger.

She spoke, very softly.

'I'm here.'

She stepped forward, into the moonlight, watching his head lift as he turned to look at her, and then, recognising her, he leaped lightly over the ground, eager to greet her. He nosed her face, and they stood, touching, his breath warm on her cheek. He had been part of her life for almost all the time she had lived here.

He pushed his head against her. She knew what he wanted and her hands cupped against his hide, the heel of her palm against his body, the fingers arched, moving in small circles, clockwise, so that the skin slid over the muscle. It was a gentle movement, a soothing touch that had restored him to health when he was tiny.

She watched the soft look steal over his eyes, the slow relaxing as he gave himself to delight. It had helped many of the injured animals brought to her in the past months.

The wind strengthened, gusting from the village. There was a scent on the air: a wood fire burning. They had

11

been tidying the fields in the farm below and the last traces blew on the wind, which had changed as she waited.

She closed her eyes, both arms round the stag's neck, gaining solace from his trust. It was impossible to describe the wild elation that dominated her when one of the wilderness creatures allowed her near.

She could not ignore the acrid tang of burning wood, the smoke stinging her eyes, or the memories it evoked. The stag was restless and she prayed he would not leave her yet. Her hands began to stroke him again. He was uneasy, sniffing the air warily, his ears never still.

He lifted his head. He had had enough of her ministrations. She stroked him rapidly, joining the circles, and he put his head down to her face again. It was his gift to her and it always thrilled her, as did the knowledge that although he had returned to his own wild life, he still visited her regularly.

When snow lay deep on the ground he rapped on the door with his hoof, asking for food as he had while he was recovering. The bond between them deepened.

He comforted her as no human could. With him at night she walked the forest rides and was unafraid. His presence beside her seemed to reassure other animals, so that she had played with fox cubs the year before and looked forward to new families soon. The deer told her if there were strangers on the hill and, if she received his warning, she followed him into hiding.

A mist was rising from the ground. They moved through it like figures in a dream. It lay low, the trees rearing like startled animals. There was a sudden thickening, and dim bodies raced through the night. The stag vanished into the bushes and Torran followed him, wondering what had alarmed the speeding hinds.

The villagers said that ghost armies thundered on Staghill. Could these be the source of such stories, or were there eerie shadows that had caused the herd to bolt?

Then she saw the reason as two feral cats appeared, as if herding them. They were intent on hunting, though their quarry was not deer.

The mist enlarged them to giant size, bigger than any known cat, insubstantial bodies that vanished like ghosts, giving birth to more legends when briefly glimpsed.

Torran walked higher up the hill, the stag beside her. They paced together below the light of a fading moon hiding among clouds that gathered darkly, threatening rain but taking away the risk of frost.

*   *   *

Two men had been watching Torran meet the stag. They turned away from the window of the old house halfway up Staghill. The room was lit by flames from logs that blazed in the huge hearth. The Colonel switched on the light, banishing illusion.

'From realms of faerie,' the schoolmaster said. The quotation eluded the Colonel. Lyan was staring through the glass, though the woods were now only a memory, no longer visible. 'I never tire of watching that first meeting.'

'Are you going out tonight?' the Colonel asked. 'I'm always happier when you're there. We never have had intruders, so far as I know. But nothing is certain in this life, as Torran knows, only too well. She doesn't seem to mind you.'

'She tolerates me. She knows I love the animals too, and we sometimes exchange a few words about the cubs, or the badgers. Sometimes about the deer.' He glanced out of the window, where darkness covered the trees, and saw only a reflection of the warm room, himself and the Colonel mirrored there. He sighed, and was suddenly moved to reveal more of himself than he had intended. 'She reminds me of the girl in that Charlotte Mew poem, "The Farmer's Bride", who fled when men came near

... "The women say that beasts in stall/Look round like children at her call./I've hardly heard her speak at all."''

He did not add the last lines, but they haunted him and had done so ever since he first saw her ... 'Oh! my God! the down,/The soft young down of her ... her eyes, her hair, her hair!' It was thick and dark and silky and would feel gossamer-fine to his touch. He should know better. He had been alone too long since his divorce.

His companion had other worries on his mind. He was used to the schoolmaster's passion for quotation, and endured it. He himself found little pleasure in poetry, feeling that men who liked it were effete. That, he had to admit, did not apply to Lyan.

As he walked over to the fireplace, intending to sit in the big leather-covered easy chair, Lyan looked at the sideboard which was covered, unusually, in bottles, some full, some half-empty.

'Are we giving a party?'

'Jan brought them over. It's the second anniversary of the massacre at their African home. They've both been skating the subject all day. Torran has her own comfort, though I'm not sure that it'll stand her in good stead today. Jan was afraid that once she had gone out, he'd find his in those. He's taken up wine-making as a hobby. Good stuff, but potent. So he brought them over to remove the temptation. He didn't want her to come home and find him drunk.'

Lyan fingered his face. Memory scarred as well as bullets, and fear had a way of surfacing at unexpected moments. He himself had, briefly, sought comfort in alcohol but learned fast that it brought more problems than it solved.

'Jan has never seemed as badly affected as Torran.'

'He was always a private man. They both saw the bodies; they heard them die. All the women were raped—her

14

large Elizabethan farmhouse, it did not really deserve the name. The estate was considerable. He was relieved to discover that though Stephanie had left no money, she had a large collection of antique jewellery that had passed from mother to daughter for several generations.

He could not believe the astonishing amount that had been raised when it was sent to Sotheby's for auction.

Within months he had developed a passion for his new home. He loved the wildness and enjoyed watching the animals. His killing days were long over and he would not even join a pheasant shoot run by past acquaintances.

His life was fully occupied as he planned to restore the woods to their former glory. He had always been a fit man, and could still outwalk many much younger than he. He attacked small portions of woodland near to the house, clearing the ground, removing dead trees, letting in light for the survivors, so that once more there were snowdrops and windflowers and daffodils and bluebells in the spring, instead of damp vegetation soured by overgrowth of trees struggling for light and air.

He had not expected to find a major interest after his retirement, but he felt, as he worked, that he was creating a new Eden, a place where a man might restore his soul, a sanctuary for the creatures that hid in the bushes. No one would hunt them or harry them on his property, though he could not stop the hounds from chasing the foxes beyond his boundaries.

During the first years he spent much of the night watching the fox cubs play in the clearings he had made, and made notes of the passage of the owls as they flew and hunted. He mapped the badger setts, learning their paths through the woods. Then arthritis claimed him and he was forced to admit that his night-time rambles were inadvisable. He resented his age and feared disability.

*   *   *

17

The village was dark now, except for one light that shone from a house beyond the church where a mother nursed a sick child. The street-lamps went out at midnight. Far away, across the valley, a train raced through the darkness, its lights bright, its shape unguessed at, giving it an uncanny appearance. The stag watched it, and Torran wondered what he made of it.

She had not eaten since lunchtime. She brought out the little pack of sandwiches from her pocket, smiling at the sudden greed that lit his eyes, and the dip of his nose against the paper, urging her to hurry and open it.

A deer that liked egg and cress sandwiches was an absurdity, but no more so than a horse that Jan had once owned who stole his roast beef and horseradish sandwiches one day, and apparently enjoyed every mouthful.

She ate part of her share and lost the rest when his longing overcame him and he snatched it from her hand.

She laughed.

'You horrible animal. You always were more like a pig than a deer, did you know that? I'd starve if you lived with me . . . stealing the food from my mouth.'

He had been adorable when she first saw him. She looked at him now, wondering if he remembered the days when he had dragged his plastered leg around, had rapped with impatience at feeding time for his bottle, using his good front leg to bang against the wood of the little shed where he slept on deep straw.

Did he remember his delight when at last the restriction was removed and he began to learn to move again? He had discovered the joy of leaping, had frisked and fussed and played with the orphan lamb that she had taken from the farm below when the ewe died, which the farmer had intended to sell for meat.

Jojo had returned to the farm when he was weaned, where he had quickly proved that he did not think of himself as a sheep. He bullied every ewe and lamb who came near, butting them away, and was defiant with the dogs, so that none could herd him. Luckily he was not horned, or he might have been really dangerous.

'I'm nuts, do you know that?' Torran asked the stag, as she shared her apple with him. A faint trace of smoke caught her nostrils and memory flared again. 'I'm dominated by a horde of idiotic animals.'

She looked down the hill. Jan left a light in the cottage all night, so that she did not have to blunder in the dark when she came home. It was a small beacon that always warmed her, as did his concern. Silver, wanting attention, nudged her with his head.

She smiled as he nosed her again, as if acknowledging what she had said.

'Maybe it's as well. Salvation comes in strange disguises, and you're one of them.'

He butted her, leaped away, and then came back to her, pushing against her hand, asking her to stroke him again.

Moonlight silvered his coat, and she put her arms around him, deriving comfort.

Two

The Colonel switched off the light. He always worried when he knew Torran was out in the woods.

The two men were unlikely companions. Lyan's father had been in the Colonel's regiment. The schoolmaster, recovering from personal tragedy, had not liked to impose himself on the Colonel and had lived in uncomfortable lodgings for nearly two years.

They had met one evening in the Dog and Duck. The Colonel recognised the unusual name and asked if Lyan were indeed the son of Jacob Grant, who had been in the same regiment as himself during the Second World War.

The two older men had remained friends. Jacob had shown photographs of his son with pride, but had died too young, of a coronary, some years before Roger retired.

The Colonel and the schoolmaster had many common interests. At the beginning of that year Roger had offered Lyan rooms in the Place, one a large bedroom with its own bathroom and the other a palatial sitting-room which housed the many books that had never been taken out of their boxes since his marriage ended.

He had accepted gladly, as his village lodging was a small room in the house of a woman so obsessed by cleanliness that he had to change into his slippers before setting foot in her hall.

'I rattle around here like a single pea in an enormous pod,' Roger Manton had said. 'The Place was built when farmers had large families and labour was cheap. I'd let off some of the other rooms too, but Mrs Burton would leave if I did. I'd enjoy company, and talk in the evenings, instead of sitting here alone. Mrs Burton has no conversation at all.'

Dorothy Burton was the widow of one of the sergeants in his old regiment, a dour woman, insistent on formality, so that neither the Colonel nor his lodger even knew her first name. She had her own domain, comprising a bedroom, sitting-room and bathroom, and ate her meals alone, keeping herself aloof from the men.

'She's a wearing woman, but a hard worker and a good cook.' The Colonel found her difficult at times, and regretted the impulse that had led him to offer her the job, solely on the basis that he had known and respected her long-dead husband.

Now he looked regretfully at the pipe that lay on the mantelpiece and which he had been persuaded to give up.

'If you keep up that dirty habit, I leave,' she had said. The Colonel doubted if he would find adequate help among the village women and was too aware that he was far from being accepted, so gave in, preferring peace in his later years to a state of constant friction.

In the few weeks that he had lived in Staghill Place Lyan had found no reason to regret his change of home. His landlord was an interesting man and they spent many hours putting the world to rights.

He walked over to the window, hoping for another glimpse of Torran and the white stag, but nothing moved.

'No wonder the villagers believe in the legend about the ghostly white stag.' The Colonel's voice was wistful. Torran and her grandfather were also his protégés. Jan Ardan had fought with the Colonel in World War Two, sharing night raids and strange adventures behind the lines, sabotaging military targets.

Lyan now knew that the Colonel surrounded himself with those in need of help. He had once been responsible for all his men and had taken his duty very seriously. A father to all his children . . . he often scolded himself for keeping up old attitudes, but they were a long-standing part of his life and he could not discard them.

The Colonel switched on the light again and voiced another worry.

'Jan said she's putting out food for the foxes. That won't be popular if Jim Cartright finds out. He's lost several chickens and two geese in the last few weeks and is vowing vengeance.'

'Would he harm her?' Lyan fingered the scar across his cheek, and turned the right side of his face away from the Colonel, who noted the gesture and sighed. Before he offered Lyan a home he had phoned another old friend, an Assistant Commissioner at Scotland Yard. He was thankful for so many connections. He had learnt the reason for the schoolmaster's coming to Lynsom Green. As yet, he had not been told by the man himself and wondered if he would ever feel able to share the burden of memory that he carried with him.

Lyan often wondered at the Colonel's almost obsessive interest in the Ardans. Few days went by without Jan visiting although Torran kept away, unwilling always to meet with strangers.

Jan helped with the outdoor work, tidying up the dead trees, willing to give his time generously without reward.

'Did you know Torran before they came here?' Lyan asked. Their respect for one another was growing into friendship, though as yet confidences were few.

'She reminds me of a fawn,' the Colonel said. 'Her mother was like that, too. Huge eyes, in a tiny face, eyes that pleaded for more than anyone could ever give her.'

'You knew her well?'

'Torran's my daughter.' He saw the startled expression on Lyan's face. 'Oh, nothing like that. I married Ginevra. It was one of those crazy alliances that are doomed from the start. I was much older than she, the dashing major,

22

and she was carried away with excitement and my obvious admiration. I had three months' leave and, having no home, spent it at a hotel in the Lake District where she was receptionist. It was middle-aged madness on my part, a glorious idiocy, only neither of us recognised that. Twenty-five years ago. I was over forty and she was only twenty-one. It was crazy. But she was sweet and I was lonely.'

He laughed ruefully, and picked up the photograph.

'This is Torran's mother.' He held it for a moment, looking at it before restoring it to its place. 'I was the typical bachelor. Do you remember the song . . . ? I've forgotten most of it, but "when he fancies he is past love, it is then he meets his last love and he loves her as he never loved before." It's so true.'

He walked over to the huge fireplace and stirred the logs with the toe of his shoe, watching the flames leap and flare. Light glinted on copper warming-pans hanging on the walls, and on the portrait of Miss Stephanie, regarding them sternly from her place above the mantelshelf. The long necklace of matched pearls, that had sold for a fortune, was round her neck. The jewels in the rings on both hands sparkled as they must have done when she was alive.

Quint and Sapphire stretched themselves to the warmth, revelling. Mrs Burton objected to their presence indoors, but this was one habit she was not going to change. Whenever she had the opportunity she took them to the outhouse beyond the kitchen where they slept. The Colonel hated leaving them in her charge, but at times had no choice.

He had not refurnished. The house was almost a museum. Lyan found it restful, though he would have preferred lighter colours and less sombre walls.

'I was too old for marriage. Ginevra expected an adoring husband who would wine her and dine her and flaunt her. Dear Heaven, she was a beauty. Honeymoons end and pregnancy came too soon. I thought she knew things that she didn't. Only then did I realise the gulf between us. She was little more than a schoolgirl, and couldn't share any of my interests.'

He paused and bent to stroke Sapphire, the older of his dogs, who had begun to nuzzle his leg. Her sharp ears flattened against her head in rapture.

'I was sent away for a year overseas with my regiment. No wives. Torran was born while I was away. Jan Ardan had only been in the army for the duration of the war. He was working for a firm near our home. He used to call on us and his wife suggested that Ginevra visit as she knew she was lonely.'

Lyan, listening, sighed, knowing the pattern only too well.

'It's odd how such a little thing as a kindness to a friend's family could result in heartbreak. Ginevra's mother was dead, her father remarried and not interested in her, and she was panicky with the baby so near. The Ardans invited her to stay. Steve, their son, fell in love. He was only two years older than she. I was far away and my letters home were few. I was a memory; he was there, ready to comfort her. I blamed Jan for the divorce for a long time. Steve and Ginevra adopted Torran and changed her surname.'

'Does she know you're her father?'

'She knew Steve wasn't her real father, but they never told her my name. She knew I had been a soldier and believed I was dead. Ginevra felt it would be better for the child. I agreed. I had never even seen the baby. She wasn't a reality.'

He stroked Sapphire absentmindedly, his hand resting lightly on the warm body. She nuzzled his wrist, loving the contact.

'We don't know how to tell her. Jan feels that she

couldn't face the knowledge now and it might turn her against me. As it is, she understands that I'm an old family friend. I never expected they would come back into my life, other than at a distance. Jan sent photographs of her and news as she grew.'

He looked back into a distant past that seemed almost a dream.

'She's so like her mother. Seeing her rouses memories, and there's a bond, even if it's never acknowledged. My child. My daughter, within such a little distance of me, and I can't tell her. She isn't recovering as she should; she needs help and neither of us knows how to give it. She won't go to a doctor. She says there's nothing wrong.'

Lyan thought of his own two children, irretrievably lost. He could force access, but they had been alienated, and he saw little virtue in visits that the children endured because the law said they must. The ache remained, and often the chance gesture of a child in his class brought back an intolerable longing.

The Colonel had to continue his story now that he had begun. He felt as if he were in a confessional and the pain of years was being exposed.

'I set up a trust for the child, only to be used in emergency. It's quite sizeable now, and will have to be explained one day. Jan is trustee. He refuses to use it, feeling it may be needed when he dies, as he has little now to leave her.'

Quint, the younger dog, suddenly jealous, roused himself, pushed the bitch away and laid his head on his master's knee, looking longingly into his eyes, asking for attention too. The Colonel smiled. They were his companions, more precious to him than anyone he knew, giving him unstinting affection. Sapphire, unwilling to challenge, went to find comfort from Lyan.

Roger Manton sighed before he continued speaking.

25

'I realised in time that it wasn't Jan's fault. Just one of those things. His wife died and he became redundant. He went out to Africa to join Steve and Ginevra. They had taken over from Jan's father, as he wasn't interested in farming.'

He glanced out at the dusky woods. There was a sudden piercing cry from a bird hidden outside the window. An owl flew by, enlarged by darkness, a silent presence, floating low in an undulating movement between the trees. The woods were a benison, enclosing the Place, the lights of the cottage showing, lower down, through the crowded branches.

'Jan had his own house, some distance away. It was a huge property. They bred cattle. They were happy until the night the farm was raided.'

'You never married again?'

'Soldiers shouldn't take wives. It's too difficult for them and their families. I paid dearly for my midlife madness. I don't think I had ever been deeply in love until I met Ginevra . . . I wanted to protect her, shelter her, keep her safe from harm. She needed that, and I failed her. It was the wrong kind of life for her.'

'Like policemen,' Lyan said, a wry smile on his face. 'My wife never did get used to the unsocial hours, to having me called away just as we were about to go out or entertain. I don't miss her. She changed. I do miss the children. I never have news of them, and often wonder how they are and what they're doing. Susie must be twelve now, and Bob will be fourteen. I doubt if I'd recognise them if I met them in the street. All maintenance is paid through my solicitor. There's no contact.'

He glanced at the door as it opened and Mrs Burton came in, a tray in her hands. Not thinking, his mind on their conversation, he walked across the room to take it from her.

'I'm not helpless,' she said, setting it down on the table

and putting the two plates on the mats. The sharp bang made both dogs look up, ears pricked, eyes wary.

She looked at the array of bottles on the sideboard, and sniffed. Both men had come to dread those sniffs.

'You'll go easy on those, if you please. I don't hold with strong drink.' She hesitated, as if unsure, and then made up her mind to speak.

'There's talk in the village.' She glared at the Colonel as if he were to blame.

'There's always talk in the village. What is it this time?'

'They say she's a witch, all that nonsense with the animals. And those brews she makes, and the way she lays her hands on the sick beasts. There's those as will take her a dog or a cat. She only sees them if they're with children. Pretends she'll have no truck with adults.' She sniffed. 'And they say he's not her grandfather. Not right them having the cottage when there's others that need it.'

No need to say who 'she' was. Dorothy Burton did not like the Ardans. She resented Lyan, and felt she had been cheated. No one had warned her that there might be two men to look after, or two large, messy dogs. She wanted her employer to herself, although she could never have explained why. Her possessiveness and her uncompromising manner had driven away both her sons. Not even Roger was aware that she had ever had a family.

The cottage belonged to the big house, and if the Ardans left she was sure she would have the right to move there. She did not like living under someone else's roof, with only two rooms to call her own. She wanted her own place.

The Colonel tried appeasement.

'No one in the village wanted the cottage. It was almost a ruin. No one would repair it and no one wanted to live in the woods halfway up Staghill, with a long walk to the shop, and no company near.'

Dorothy Burton sniffed again, picked up the empty tray and walked out, closing the door decisively behind her. Quint growled. The housekeeper refused to feed the dogs or care for them and he was aware of her attitude and showed it. Sapphire, more trusting, tried her best to win approval and could never understand why she failed.

The Colonel looked at the two plates and changed them over.

'She's never learnt that you have a much bigger appetite than I. Or do you think she does it on purpose?'

Lyan grinned. He was learning that the housekeeper disliked him intensely, though her ways of showing it were subtle. He took care to keep out of her way as much as possible. His room was always immaculate. He made his own bed, but she did condescend to change the sheets.

'I suspect she thinks I live here rent free, and that you're lying when you say I more than pay my way.' He cut into a roast potato. 'She's probably convinced the Ardans sponge off you and also live rent free.' He paused. The meat was tender, the vegetables well flavoured, the sauce unusual. 'She is a good cook.'

'So long as she doesn't try cakes. I had the greatest job dissuading her. Her sponges are like leather and her rock cakes more solid than granite. Even the birds ignore them.' He laughed. 'I watched a blackbird try to break one into pieces and finally give up. Her husband was a good man. But soldiers don't leave large pensions, and she was in the most miserable bedsit I've seen for a long time. I haven't the heart to condemn her to that again, but I do wish she'd try and be civil on occasion.'

'Maybe she hopes you'll marry her,' Lyan said, a mischievous grin on his lips.

'God save us,' the Colonel said when he had regained his breath and stopped spluttering. 'Don't even suggest such a thing.'

'I think that's why she resents me. She had hoped you'd

need her company. Instead we sit and talk man-talk, and she has no place.'

'She kept to her own rooms even before you came.' The Colonel cut the last potato on his plate in two. The dogs came to sit beside him, tongues out, drooling. He laughed and gave each a share. 'All the same, I'm worried. She makes me uneasy and I don't know why.'

'You don't have to marry her. Maybe she aims at being a common-law wife, which the village is probably sure she is already. Does it bother you?'

'Oh that . . . There's no chance. No. It's the Ardans. I wouldn't put it past the villagers to set up some kind of campaign to try and drive them away. That's what I meant when I said I came here for peace, and there doesn't seem to be such a thing.'

'How could they do that?'

'I think it's already begun. Jan called on me earlier today, and gave me this. Maybe we need to take it to the police. I don't know. It could be children. I wasn't going to tell you, but I think I need your help.'

He handed over a lined sheet of paper which might well have come from a school class-book. It was a centre page, pulled out cleanly, leaving the marks of the staples that had held it in place.

Lyan read the neat, characterless capitals with distaste:

GO BACK WHERE YOU BELONG. YOU AREN'T WANTED HERE, NOT YOU NOR THE WITCH WOMAN. WE ALL KNOW SHE ISN'T YOUR GRANDDAUGHTER. THE WHITE STAG HAS MARKED HER FOR DEATH. BEWARE!

He mentally reviewed the villagers, and the children. 'Joe McToul?'

'He can't write. In any case, he's so simple I don't think

such thoughts would occur to him. I often wonder if he has any thoughts.'

'Then who?'

'It's meant to scare . . . not as a threat of future action,' the Colonel said, but he didn't sound convinced. 'Jan and I are both agreed that Torran mustn't know. She's only just beginning to heal. Keep your eyes open when you're out in the woods at night. You never know who's about.'

'I'll watch,' Lyan said, and prayed that he would never need to act, as he was sure he no longer had the courage to challenge anyone who might cause harm. The mere thought of a violent confrontation made him shudder. He stroked his hand down the scar on his face, remembering the agony of torn flesh and the long months of painful recovery.

He was startled by the anger he felt at the thought of his refuge being invaded by brutality from the outside world. The Colonel picked up his cup of coffee, walked over to the window, and looked out at the moon-dappled trees.

'There's danger in that note,' he said. 'I don't like to think there's someone out there, checking. There's no harm at all in either of them. She's as much Jan's granddaughter as her half-sisters, Lysbeth and Nerine, and even dearer now they're both gone.'

Lyan found himself thinking of days long ago, when he had been in the police, and of the trouble caused by anonymous letters, bringing fear to communities, hinting at sins that had never been committed, in some cases causing death.

The two dogs were watching their master, waiting for him to put down his cup, knowing that when he did so they would be off for a walk in the woods and a last romp before bedtime. Sapphire beat her tail on the ground, and Quint sat alert, longing to be noticed.

The Colonel paced the room, unable to sit still.

'Staghill's enabled me to give my daughter a home. It's given me a new interest. I know the animals that live here; I know something about their lives, and I intend to protect them, whatever happens, as I do Jan and Torran.'

He moved away from the hearth.

'Nobody is going to harm them, nor are they leaving. I'll take very good care of that.'

The dogs were watching intently, heads raised, eyes puzzled by the atmosphere in the room. They sensed discord and did not know why. Uneasily, Sapphire stood and stretched and walked over to her master, looking up searchingly into his face, as if asking him what was wrong. He stroked her shoulder and she leaned against him, more sensitive than Quint to human emotions.

'I may be stupid but I do so very much hope that one day we'll be able to tell Torran and she'll acknowledge me. I love her far more than I ever did her mother, though in a completely different way. That love died, as I felt betrayed, though I know now I asked too much of Ginevra.' He picked up the empty pipe and looked at it, and put it back again on the mantelshelf with a sigh. 'The more I see of Torran, the more I want her to know she's mine.'

The dogs waited, becoming increasingly impatient. Sapphire whined, anxious for her walk, and the Colonel picked up the leads.

* * *

Out in the woods Torran watched on, knowing sleep would either elude her or bring terrifying dreams if she returned home now. She was seated on a fallen tree trunk, the stag beside her, always alert. Fear almost paralysed as she heard an extraordinary sound nearby, reminding her of her younger sister who, when small, had loved to rattle a stick along some iron railings that bordered their property.

She relaxed as she realised that it was a bat, its wings flickering among the branches above her. The stag raised his head to look and then settled again, waiting beside her. The moon appeared briefly between racing clouds, driven by a rising wind building to a gale. She glimpsed a feral cat in the shadows, heavily pregnant, treading warily, anxious not to be seen.

Time to return. She walked down the hill. There was a voice from below as Jim Cartwright went to milk and called to his sleepy son to bestir himself. The wind carried the voices. The stag, startled, was gone. She watched until he vanished among the trees. Like her, he was almost always alone. She lived with Jan, yet they could not communicate at all, each appreciating the other's need yet unable to satisfy it.

The peace she had hoped for eluded her. The wind in the trees sobbed and sighed and sang, and there were other strange noises in the night. She had to forget. There was work to be done and perhaps in that she could lose herself completely. The animals needed her.

The day before the vet had brought an injured squirrel for her to nurse. She wondered if the little creature had survived the night. He had been caught by a cat and had several bad bites. She knew from experience that he would not be an easy patient. She had a scar on her finger to prove it, from a female that had given birth while in the tiny animal hospital that Jan had built for her.

Jan was waiting for her. He always worried when she went out at night, but knew that her forays were therapy. He was eternally grateful to the Colonel for offering them a refuge.

He was a slight man, lean and active in spite of his seventy years. Thick grey hair and a small Vandyke beard lent his face a distinction that was enhanced by unusually elongated green eyes, which glittered when he was happy. Her half-sisters had inherited them, and she saw them, often, when she looked at him. Time healed grief, they said. She did not believe them.

Dawn was adding colour to the world as she walked slowly up the track towards the cottage. Jan sighed with relief and turned away. He did not see her stop and stare at the envelope pinned to the door.

The address was printed in block capitals: 'TO THE WOMAN AT STAGHILL COTTAGE'.

She took it down, removing the drawing-pin. Her ears had not deceived her: she *had* heard human movement in the woods. Her sanctuary had been invaded. The thought of that worried her almost more than the paper in her hand. What sort of message was inside? She thrust it deep into her pocket and greeted Jan with a smile and a kiss.

'Did Silver come?' he asked.

'Yes. He's well, and as mischievous as ever. He took a button off my coat again. I'll have to make sure I wear zips. I wonder if he could undo those?'

He laughed.

'There's a hot drink in the flask. I'm off to my bed now I know you're safe.'

Am I? she wondered anxiously as he left the room. She tore open the envelope. The words mocked her:

GO BACK WHERE YOU BELONG. NOBODY WANTS YOUR KIND HERE. WE ALL KNOW WHAT YOU DO AT NIGHT WITH THE MEN YOU MEET. WE KNOW WHY YOU CAME TO WITCH COTTAGE.

She felt sick. Who hated her so much? Whatever happened, Jan must not know. She watched the letter and envelope fall to ash among the burning logs, and knew

33

that now, more than ever, she would be afraid of those hostile eyes that stared at her when she passed.

Who?

Three

The anonymous letter that Roger Manton had shown him worried Lyan. It bothered him all the next day. That night, when he went to bed, sleep eluded him.

He had been a policeman for twenty years, and he sensed malice. He himself was finding a fragile confidence again, although his scarred face still caused him misery when eyes that looked at him looked away again, upset by its presence.

Lying awake, the pattern repeated itself in his head. He knew only too well how Jan and Torran felt: he too had been the victim of undeserved viciousness.

He had started his adult life in the police force. He became one of those who carried guns when needed. The night when a bank robber shot at him, he had not been quick enough. He had endured months of operations, but even with all the surgeon's skill, he was still scarred. It was a miracle, they said, that he had not lost his sight.

Recovery was slow, and when at last he returned to duty he had lost his nerve. The following weeks saw a slow deterioration and then a complete breakdown; he spent almost a year in hospital, trying to recover his former confidence. His wife, impatient, could not understand the change in him. During the time he was away from her she found consolation elsewhere. Her new partner worked normal hours and could give her companionship without being suddenly called away.

She left Lyan, taking their two children with her.

Therapy for him came, unexpectedly, in the books of poetry lent by a teacher friend, who had been at school with him. He never failed to visit each week, and bring more books. No one else ever came to see him during those long months. He discovered a forgotten fascination with words and a passion for language. When at last he was discharged he did not need much persuasion to re-train, and to teach.

He chose the school in Lynsom Green because the village was remote from town and city bustle and he pre-ferred country children and a rural life. In the two-and-a-half years he had lived there he had become as passionate as the Colonel about Staghill and the animals that hid in the woods.

His night-time forays were much easier now that he lived in the Place. His landlady had been suspicious and he suspected that she thought he was conducting an illicit liaison, though he did not know who she imagined was the other partner in his sin. He hoped it was not Torran who, unwittingly, provided her with fuel for her imagination.

Sleep seemed farther away than ever. The anonymous letter was a sign of a disturbed mind. He could not chan-nel his thoughts. He dressed again and went out into the darkness, taking his camera. The woods were his route to sanity.

He stood beneath the trees, feeling the wind on his cheek, and hearing the small noises of the night as the animals went about their business. There under the stars he felt his own unimportance, and thought of a world that had been in existence long before he was born and would continue long afterwards, relegating him to an atom in the universe.

The badgers were foraging at the edge of the stream. He filmed them, with only half his mind on his work. The big boar was rooting for food. The female, bustling like a plump housekeeper, lined her sett with bracken which she cut with her teeth and then gathered with her forepaws, dragging her bedding backwards and making the oddest shuffling noises.

Moonlight shone on black and white stripes. The wind blew towards Lyan and he remained unseen and unscented. The boar was used to him and might come close, but the sow was timid and backed away. Often her small head appeared in the opening of her sett and she looked out, only to dive back into darkness, to summon her courage before venturing again into the woods. A footstep sent her speeding along the path, to the safety of her underground home.

He sat in his favourite place, on a fallen tree whose branches were sprouting again. Below him the village houses were humped in the faint moonlight, here and there a light showing where someone sat with a crying child or an invalid. He knew most of the parents of the children who came to the school. He knew also that the villagers had little time for outsiders, or 'incomers', as the postmistress called them. He had not been noticed the day the Ardans moved in, as he waited to buy stamps.

'Should have gone to someone in the village. And the new schoolmaster's from outside.' Effie Green said 'out-side' as if it were an unspeakable place. 'Soon be no room for us at all. Too many incomers coming to live here.'

He recalled the conversation now. It did not occur to him that his police training was dictating his line of thought. He reviewed odd items of gossip that he had heard and facts he had gleaned from the children. They often amused him with their odd ideas.

Staghill had been a place of legend and mystery for as long as the village of Lynsom Green had sheltered below it. There, long ago, it was said, battles had been fought and ghost legions still came out to face men who lay in ambush. There, over the centuries, many young men had left their blood, and women had wept over the bodies of those who would never come home again.

Joe McToul, who had fewer wits in his head than a three-year-old child, swore that he had seen the armies marching at night, the warriors riding out, brave with banners and beating drums. In the morning, the tattered remnants dragged their way back, men bandaged, women wailing, one drum thumping a death march. Yet when the mist cleared there was nothing to be seen, and there were no footsteps in the dew.

There, two centuries ago, in the cottage which the Ardans now inhabited, had lived a witch woman. Her neighbours swore that she made evil spells and ensured that her wicked ways earned her death at the stake. The village had rejoiced at her punishment.

She had a black cat as a familiar and was often seen caressing a pure white stag who was, Effie insisted, the dark spirit of Staghill from which the place got its name. Effie was in her early sixties, busy, unmarried, sure she had been put on earth to help other people, unaware that her assistance was often regarded as intrusion and her care for others as meddling.

She was insensitive to the feelings of other people and her tongue often led her into indiscretions, leaving a trail of hurt behind her, of which she had no idea. Nobody dared tell her. She would have been horrified had she realised that she was inflicting wounds.

'Tell the truth and shame the devil' was one of her favourite sayings.

She had a lively imagination and a vast interest in the old stories of the village and its inhabitants, especially that of the eighteenth-century witch who had lived in the Ardans' cottage and had died for her beliefs. Maybe Effie wrote the letter, Lyan thought.

Staghill might be part of the Colonel's estate, but the villagers regarded it as their property, although few ever chose to walk up the hill. Children played on the outskirts, but seldom strayed far into the trees. Daring lovers, desperate for privacy, might venture farther. Few intruded into its depths.

Here foxes thrived, stags roared in the autumn, badgers foraged and played and fought, and the spring was alive with new birth. Rabbits flourished, and so did stoats and weasels. A small colony of cats, once domesticated but now so wild that few ever saw them, also haunted the hill.

Among them were coal-black cats who were, the villagers believed, descended from the beast owned by the long-ago witch woman, and were not bringers of good luck, but harbingers of evil.

Years before, the last gamekeeper had died, and nobody realised that he owned two cats, one black and white, the other black, with not one single white hair in her dense fur. They escaped to the high top, away from the noisy and terrifying people who suddenly invaded their quiet home and took away all the furniture, as well as the master they had loved.

He had lived on in his cottage, the witch cottage, long after retirement, as the estate was no longer managed. Miss Stephanie, too old to care, had given up. The cats bred and so did their progeny, although life was hard and the kittens often fell victim to prowling weasels, to the hawks that soared above the tree-tops, to other hunters that took an opportunity and decimated the little broods.

The wily thrived and the foolish died, which was also true of the fox cubs that played in the glades and learned by experience that only the strongest survived, and those most obedient to their mothers' teaching. The badgers had fewer enemies, though the farmers hated them, sure that they brought tuberculosis to their cattle.

The villagers were superstitious, few of them educated beyond the lowest school-leaving age. The most persistent legend was that of the white stag that had appeared throughout the centuries, his coming foretelling disaster, change and death.

To add to the myth, baffling those who knew little about

deer, he was always a hummel. Lyan, like the old game-keeper, suspected that white colouring and the lack of antlers went together, just as did deafness in blue-eyed white cats, or in white Boxers with one brown eye and one blue. Silver, he knew, was not deaf.

He had never seen a white female on the hill. He did not mix with the villagers, so they knew nothing of his theory and the mystery of the white antlerless stag remained unexplained. Lyan had recognised the deer for what he was. He asked the children to write about him. They had heard so many stories from their parents.

Some of the adults said he was a living animal but others, especially Joe McToul, were sure he was a ghost creature, a terrifying demon from hell. When Joe came breathless into the Dog and Duck one evening, shouting that he had seen the devil beast and a witch woman with him, there were those who believed him.

Lyan had been startled, having never before lived in such a small community. Lynsom Green was an odd place, islanded in time, with the modern world still remote. The one bus a week which took its passengers twenty miles into Pyneton was often half-empty, and for many their greatest adventure was a coach journey to Birmingham, over ninety miles away. The tiny station had been closed in the early railway cutdowns.

The churchyard was full of the relatives of those who belonged in the village, the repetition of names down the years revealing how few of the families moved out.

They resented incomers, and there were those who had come to Lynsom Green, even sixty years ago, who were still referred to as 'the man from London', or 'the woman from Lincoln', much as others might have said that the newcomer was from Greece or Spain or Italy, an alien among them.

*   *   *

The badgers had vanished and nothing else moved. A moth brushed his face. A fox yapped suddenly, close but invisible. Lyan settled himself against a tree, and continued to review the people in the village. Somebody was responsible for that letter.

He could discount the incomers. The village policeman had been born in Devon. Donald Trent, the vicar, at first resented but now accepted, came from Sussex. His wife, Melissa, from Cornwall, was too exotic for the village, with city ways, they said, and a liking for clothes that no village woman would ever wear. None of them were likely candidates.

The vicar's wife fascinated Lyan. He had never met anyone like her, and thought that her husband was a very lucky man. His landlady had disapproved of her and told him how she had shocked them when mini-skirts first came into fashion, and even more when she came to church wearing a leather jacket and skirt. Effie Green boasted that never, in all her sixty-four years, had she worn a pair of trousers, as if that were a major virtue that few women now possessed.

Melissa was rarely seen in a skirt, except on Sundays when she did conform and sit in her pew at church, planning her next foray to the antique fairs where she often picked up a bargain and re-sold it later, adding to their meagre income.

Nobody knew of these excursions, as she took care never to let anyone see her purchases, which were always small. She specialised in silver, and had a knack of finding a treasured piece in a car boot sale, wondering at the ignorance of those who sold it.

She had met her husband at a village fête, years before they came to Lynsom Green. Her mother had persuaded her to take a stall. The young curate came to buy and stayed to talk. He sometimes felt he had been bewitched that day as her face haunted him, and he at last summoned

41

up enough courage to invite her to come for a walk.

Melissa admitted only to herself that it had been his voice that enchanted her. In her private diary she named him Orpheus: he could charm the birds from the trees with his singing. When they sat together in the woods and he read poetry to her, she listened, knowing that even if she tired of him, she would never tire of that wonderful deep voice. She shut her eyes and was transported.

Sitting, not listening to his sermons, she let the tones wash over her, and felt rested. When she was very tired he sang to her, and afterwards she forgave him for all his faults. They should have had children, he would have sung wonderful lullabys; but that never happened, and perhaps as well, she thought in her more rational moments. He was a grown-up child himself, in need of constant care. If she were not there he even forgot to eat.

Melissa was one of the few people whom Lyan could meet without discomfort, as her eyes dwelled on his face and did not look hastily away, embarrassed by the scarring. He had first met her when she came to visit the Colonel with whom she had become friends when the jewellery was sold. She had been as delighted as if it were her own. He offered her a commission fee which she refused.

They were the only people in the village who knew of her dealing, and she often came up to talk, or show them some pretty object she had found in her travels.

She had come one night when the Colonel was playing an old Paul Robeson cassette.

'He sounds just like Donald . . . deep velvet,' she said, and, after two glasses of wine which she knew she ought not to have drunk, as it always went straight to her head, had told them of her courtship. Lyan, who had wanted to spend the night badger-watching and restricted his drinking to mineral water, drove her home in the little old runabout that he cared for devotedly. They sat outside the vicarage listening to the vicar singing to himself.

The village choir were rehearsing *The Mikado,* with Donald playing the Lord High Executioner. Lyan, hearing the magical voice, could well imagine that any woman would be entranced, especially if its owner were dedicated to singing only to her. Neither she nor the vicar would write anonymous letters.

He needed to know more about the villagers, to overcome his reluctance to meet them in his daily life. Perhaps the children could provide some clues. They had given him very odd glimpses when asked to write about the most exciting thing that had ever happened to them.

Mark Luton had produced a story about riding a bolting horse, and suddenly finding himself on a racecourse, winning the race. Lucy Cartwright had seen the ghost army pouring down the hill and had run home in terror with the ghosts pursuing her.

'As I past the barn,' she had written, 'a grate cold hand closed round my throte and I thoght I wood die.' She had apparently run out of ideas as the account ended there.

Shannon Prince had flown on a magic rug that her mother had bought from a bent old lady in exchange for two balloons left over from a party. Tom Lincoln's father was apparently being sought by the police, having robbed a bank and stolen a car and run away from home.

Lyan grinned to himself on reading the account, as Paul Lincoln, a mild man hidden behind enormous horn-rimmed glasses, was one of the partners in a solicitors' office in Pyneton and most certainly was not away from home: they had met that evening and nodded to one another.

Davey Prentice had written about his father who was, he said, 'a very important man, and as well was a local counseler who had lots of bisineses.' They were going to Bermuda for their holiday and they had been to Florida the year before. He had spelt both of those correctly.

There was a small wind rising and clouds were darkening the moon. None of the animals seemed to be stirring, though high on the hill he heard the snarl and swear of two fighting cats. Owls were calling, but he had seen nothing.

He indulged himself in a fantasy. His filming was so good that he sold not only to the BBC or ITV, but also to many other countries. Staghill had so much to offer, when the animals chose to co-operate.

He stood, looking down on a village where only one light shone in a bedroom window. As he watched, it went out. All the world was asleep and he alone was awake.

Nobody down there knew how it felt to lie restless, with racing thoughts, a mind in turmoil. Maybe one day he would sleep again. He had a sudden memory of saying bitterly to one of his doctors, 'Sleep is something that other people do.'

He could not remember the man's name. He had been middle-aged, with greying hair and round glasses over huge brown eyes that gave him the look of a meditative owl. It was he who had suggested that instead of lying frustrated and angry, Lyan should get up and find something to do with the night-time hours. It was the best piece of medical advice he had ever been given.

He had not so far seen Torran that night. His mind was filled with odd lines of poetry whenever he met her. His diary was filled with poems that he wrote to her. She was, at least, not afraid of him, knowing he shared her passion for animals. He did not need to hide his scarred face from her, as they only met in the dark. If the moon shone full he kept to the shadows.

Her face haunted him. He saw it when he lay down to sleep. He saw it at times when he was correcting the children's work. He knew now why she reminded him of the photograph in the Colonel's study. The two women had the same eyes and delicate bone structure.

He wished she would come, but the woods covered

44

many acres and she could well be hidden from him higher on the hill. He had captured her and the white stag with his camera. She was an image to be cherished, reminding him of legends of virgins who tamed unicorns so that the splendid beasts laid their trusting heads in the maidens' laps. Not even the Colonel knew of his second film, though he saw those of the animals.

'You'd never guess there were so many,' he had commented one day, two weeks before, as he showed the Colonel footage of fox and badger, a little herd of deer and a cruising owl. The bird had floated out of the darkness, swooping to reappear from the long grass with a rat in his mouth as he winged away to his nest to feed his hungry babies.

Torran had watched him that night, the white stag near, but hidden in the undergrowth, waiting for Lyan's departure.

'They know we won't hurt them,' she said, as he put away the camera. 'We're part of their landscape and never threaten them. I'm glad they stay wary of others. I'm always afraid they might be harmed.'

He hoped that in time Silver would also accept him, and accompany him when he was out in the woods. Perhaps then Torran would favour him more often with her own companionship. Their meetings were brief and she had little to say. At least she no longer hid when he was there.

His thoughts ranged as he waited. The sky was overcast, with only a hint of moonlight between the passing clouds, and a faint rain was beginning. Perhaps she would not come at all in such weather.

He thought of the lessons he would give next day, the legends he would tell of Staghill and its animals. One day he might write them down, make them into a book, if only he could capture his own enchantment and turn it into words.

He loved story-telling. Those were the times when the children sat absorbed and listened, not even the naughtiest playing the fool.

Tonight the woods failed to soothe his uneasiness. There was malice in that letter. Below him lay the village, a tangle of narrow lanes that twisted among fields of rape and corn and barley and browsing cattle and flocks of sheep. The land around it was interspersed with isolated farmhouses.

Who could the writer be?

The postmistress who ran the only shop, and sold newspapers and magazines, oddments that might be useful, as well as most of the staples needed. It was a mixture of grocer and greengrocer, of post office and chemist, with sweets for the children and an off licence for the adults, a fact that annoyed the landlord of the Dog and Duck. Surely not her.

Could it be one of the Cartwrights at the farm that lay at the foot of Staghill? Or Pat Murphy at the garage? Was it a man or a woman?

His back ached and he moved down the glade, seeking to ease stiff legs. Moonlight glittered briefly on the church's slender spire. Mark Luton had written that God lived in that soaring steeple. An odd child, but very interesting.

The village was full of small feuds, which Mrs Burton occasionally revealed to them. She hated Gracie Lea, the postmistress.

'Overcharges. Poor-quality stock. The fruit and vegetables are never fresh and you have to watch the sell-by dates.' It added to her martyrdom as she had to take the bus to Pyneton if she wanted better produce.

Neither Lyan nor the Colonel could stand her company for the journey to and from the town, so they shopped according to her lists, making sure they stayed away all day as otherwise she would have insisted she came with them.

She thought little of their skill at finding top-quality food.

His review of the villagers had told him nothing. He could not imagine any of them producing such venom. Yet somebody had. They had to stop it. He could ask the postman if he had seen any envelopes with addresses written in block capitals among those he delivered. Lyan did not know if it had actually gone through the post.

He wondered if the letter was childish mischief, though it did not sound like children. Was it a real threat and, if so, what could they do to prevent harm coming to Torran and Jan?

Four

The vixen and the dog fox had hunted together throughout the winter. Torran brooded over them, fearing for them, as did Lyan, afraid that those who hated them might harm them. This was a young vixen. Blacktip had lost his first mate to the hounds the year before. He had, up to then, led a charmed life. He had entertained the hunt followers one autumn day when he raced after the pack, well behind them, but plainly in sight. They were on the vixen's trail and as she began to falter he yipped suddenly, long and loud, turning the trailing hound, who bayed and followed him with the rest in pursuit.

He led them over rough ground, up a rocky gully, down the hillside at breakneck speed, across a ditch and into Jim Cartwright's biggest field, racing through the browsing cattle, earning hatred as hounds and huntsmen followed, stampeding the cows. At the edge of the field he rolled in the cow-pats, coating his fur, masking his own scent.

Up on his feet fast as the lead hound almost reached him, he drove a gap through the hedge, followed by panting eager bodies, and the horsemen cleared the gate and started off after him, the pack in full cry. Jim stored another grievance to add to many.

The fox knew the hidden trails well, having been drilled by his mother when only a half-grown cub. He had escaped three times and was fast and wily, well able to hold his own. There was a twisting path through dense bracken and bramble that led to the edge of the stream. There had been rain for days and the level was high. He dived into the gap behind the waterfall that spilled from the Top Pool to the Fairy Glen, and they lost his scent.

The vixen, given a respite, escaped and hid higher up the hill.

That winter they had courted in the snow, unaware they had an audience. Lyan, watching, cuddled down behind a hedge. He filmed them as they sported, heady with joy, chasing one another in mazy circles, the vixen leaping away and then enticing the big dog fox, bowing to him, reminding the watcher of a bitch he had once owned.

The vixen raced on to a small plank bridge that crossed a stream where children played when their parents brought them to picnic. She stood in the centre, her face merry. The dog fox ran up to her and nosed her, and she, not yet ready for his advances, turned and kicked out with both hind legs, toppling him into the stream. He emerged and shook himself, the bright drops flying in the moonlight. The bedraggled and disappointed animal slipped miserably away to dry himself.

Lyan laughed. The vixen ran off the bridge into the glade, vanishing as if she had never been there at all. Two nights later they were playing happily together again. The big handsome male, his thick brush black tipped, nosed his small mate gently, rubbing against her side, pushing at her with his head, coaxing her provocatively. At last she accepted him and they vanished together at the far side of the glen, disappearing into thick undergrowth.

Lyan saw them often during the next few nights. The snow lay for almost a week and they spent the time playing together, romping in the drifts, kicking up snow behind them, rolling and diving at one another, frisky as two cubs.

He begrudged the time he had to spend away from the hill. The foxes fascinated him. If the film were a success he could give up teaching, and make more of them. He enjoyed his subject but the children exhausted him and it was always very difficult to keep their interest. He found teaching more draining than police work had been.

The weather grew bitter, clear skies bringing an Arctic chill. The little waterfall froze. One night, when the moon was high and the frost biting hard, the dog fox, running too close to the edge, slipped and slid down to the lower pool, landing on ice and skidding onto the bank. The vixen followed, and the pair amused Lyan for almost half an hour as they raced one another to the top, at times floundering in the snow, and careered down again, ending in a flurry of rolling bodies and eager, open mouths, panting like dogs as they played.

That night Torran watched too, coming like a wraith flitting through the half-light, crouching so still that the vixen took food from the bowl at her feet. The wind soothed her cheek, the touch of a wet nose enthralled her, so that she felt as if she were no longer human but part of the wild, ready to run and hide at the sound of an alien footfall.

Even the feral cats trusted her, knowing that when food was scarce she would have bowls waiting for them at the cottage, though none came near enough for her to stroke.

The dog fox watched from a distance, and then approached, allowing her to stroke his chest, tickling it with a scratching movement in the way that other folk soothed their dogs.

Lyan captured the scene on film, to look at when alone, and re-live what seemed to him a truly magical experience.

'You won't use the bits with me in them?' Torran asked. 'I don't mind you seeing; you see us anyway. But I wouldn't like to feature in a TV documentary.'

'I promise not to use them,' Lyan said. 'I like to have a record. It shows another side to the animals. Maybe if everyone respected them as you and I do, they'd show themselves far more often.'

Torran smiled at the moon.

'I'm selfish. I like to think they're mine . . . and nobody

else shares them but you. Silver is near us; one night he'll stand to meet you, but he's still wary. Jim Cartwright was on the hill a couple of weeks ago with his gun. He shot a hare. Silver saw him; he's even more suspicious of men now.'

That was a new worry. Jim hated the foxes. Would he harm the stag? He did not voice his fear.

'I can't wait for dusk,' Torran said. 'I never fail to feel excited when Silver comes to meet me. He behaves like a dog when we're alone, following me everywhere.'

Lyan knew that excitement, which he too felt when the deer and the woman met; when the night-time creatures came out and played and he was able to capture them with his camera. He forgot his scarred face when he was in the woods with Torran.

'Blacktip and Elf have been courting,' she said. 'There should be cubs soon.'

The tip of the fox's tail was black. That was an obvious name.

'Why Elf?' Lyan asked. The night was very still and they spoke in whispers.

'She's so dainty when she pounces, almost fairylike.' She laughed suddenly, the first time that Lyan had heard her do so. 'I couldn't call her Fairy, could I? Not these days.'

There was a rustle from the bushes and he held his breath as Silver came to stand behind his rescuer, almost as if on guard. He watched the schoolmaster, his ears listening, moving constantly, ready to bolt at any alien sound or sudden movement, but Torran trusted this man, and so could he.

Lyan had not seen the deer so close before and marvelled at him, at his size and strength and his gentleness. He gleamed like silver in the moonlight.

There were times when Lyan felt that Torran too was poised for flight. She knew the alarm calls as well as did the beasts that made them: the thump of a rabbit's hind leg, the flash of a white scut as the lead hind ran, the booming gonglike call of an outraged pheasant at dawn, perhaps telling them that there was a roving cat in the woods.

That was often followed by an agitated chirping and twittering and yakkering as bird after bird passed on the warning cries. She wondered if they were saying 'cat', or 'weasel', or 'hawk' by day, or 'owl' by night.

Lyan had come to treasure their meetings, and a night that passed without seeing Torran or the stag was desolate indeed.

Five

The days passed. Elf grew heavy and slow. Blacktip stayed with her and watched over her jealously. He was a swift hunter, so cunning that she fed well and the cubs inside her thrived. Torran added to their diet, but it was never enough and the dog fox began to forage farther.

Lyan hoped the pair would remain unseen. His hope was vain as Blacktip, hungry himself and aware that his mate needed more than he was providing, raided the hen-coops on Jim's farm. Jim knew they needed repair, but there was never time.

He lay in wait, one bright moonlit night, with his gun. Blacktip slipped over the wall, dropping on to the path that led to the hen-coop, knowing that he could easily break in through the inadequately fixed planks.

The shot did not kill the fox outright. He ran, looking for sanctuary in his own den. Long before he reached it he fell, exhausted, and lay with his blood slowly pumping from him. Lyan found the cold body in the early dawn. He looked down at it with anger, bitterly regretting the loss of so handsome an animal.

Blacktip would never again come to feed from Torran's bowl, or play with the vixen by the waterfall. He wondered how she would fare, robbed of the mate who would have provided food for her and her cubs.

He did not know who had fired, but suspected Jim, who had vowed vengeance often enough in the Dog and Duck where he sat, drinking too much and nursing his grievances, until he was thrown out.

Torran, finding Blacktip's body later, felt a deep sorrow

and a passionate hatred of the man who had killed him. She sat beside him, stroking the soft fur, unable to stop the tears that flooded. Her sanctuary had been invaded and would never be so safe again.

To add to her distress, there had been another anonymous letter the night before, accusing her of being responsible for the death of a calf on Jim Cartwright's farm, using her spells and potions. Again, she burned it, hoping there would be no action against them. Even if she told Jan, there was nothing anyone could do. She did not know that in this country she could ask the police for help.

Jan, worried by her absence, found her and persuaded her to come home. He buried the body at the end of the garden where lay other victims of accidents, who had not survived despite devoted nursing. The nightmares returned and Jan felt helpless, unable to comfort her.

The vixen, waiting for her mate, went to look for him. The only traces were the smells that lay on the ground where he had died. She searched the hill, but there was no sign of him. She lay, grieving, aware that now she must hunt for herself. She fared badly in the next few days, as the cubs were near to term and their weight hindered her. Even the slowest rabbit escaped and the mice were too fast for her, as she misjudged each pounce.

She fed on potatoes, left behind when the crop was lifted, turnips put out for the sheep, earthworms and beetles that she scraped out of the ground, an easier task now that the frosts had gone. She hungered for meat. She was too hampered to travel far in her search for food.

Knowing that she would be suffering, Torran put plates of dogfood near the rock that she thought sheltered the den. Elf began to rely on them. Lyan shot two rabbits and left them near, taking care to visit only when Torran had gone.

Ric was born on a starry night at the end of April. It

was a late litter, but the warmer weather helped her. Outside the deep earth the wind howled, and thunder rumbled ominously. The den itself was protected by a thicket of bramble, too dense for a man to penetrate.

He was the biggest of the four cubs, and the most vigorous. Had he not been so strong and struggled so fiercely to be born, his mother might not have brought him into the world at all.

Blind and deaf, he used his sensitive nose to scent her milk, and her dense fur gave him warmth. He curled beneath her, and she licked him, savouring her new-born cubs with delight. They slept and she lay, feeling the small bodies tucked close against her, and the soft whispering murmur that came from her was almost a purr. They comforted her, for she had lain the past few nights grieving for her lost mate.

When the cubs were five days old two leather-coated men walked at night with their Jack Russells, looking for sport and profit in the weeks to come. They had heard Tom McToul, on one of his rare trips to Pyneton market, telling a chance acquaintance in the Merry Mummer of the white deer that heralded death and the witch woman who walked with her arm around the ghost animal. Tom had little more sense at times than his brother, especially when high-flown with too much beer.

The men did not believe in ghosts. Where there was one deer there would be others. Venison commanded a high price on the black market. They prospected several times, unseen by either Lyan or Torran. They left the dogs in the van the first time they came and saw the vixen making her way home in the light of dawn. They knew where she hid.

They were not skilled woodmen, and had been lucky. On their next trip both Torran and Lyan heard them, heard the dogs, and smelled the smoke from their cigarettes. Lyan worried. Suppose they dropped a lighted fag-end? He melted into the bushes, making his way down the path in the opposite direction, knowing it would be unwise to risk an encounter. He hoped that Torran was not visiting the wood that night.

Silver warned her with a sudden stamp, a butt of his nose against her side, and a quick disappearance into the bushes. Hidden high in a tree, she held her breath, praying that the intruders would not find the vixen and harm her.

She relived terror, seeing flames and hearing screams and the appalling shouting and laughter. God give me strength, she prayed, afraid she might fall and bring the poachers after her.

She was aware of the bowl of food, a tell-tale that the two might not miss, and thought of the dead dog fox. Why couldn't men leave the wild creatures alone? Her heart was beating so loudly she was sure the dogs would hear her. Hopefully they would not catch her scent. The men had heavy sticks, but not guns. The terriers were the chief danger.

She quivered with fear as the dogs paused beneath her tree, noses lifted, scenting the air, but their owners, impatient, whistled them on. Foxes didn't live in trees and they thought the pair had smelt squirrels. They were after more rewarding prey.

They were unaware that their thumping feet and their unruly companions had alerted every animal within range, and that the hillside was filled with hidden creatures, listening and waiting, fear dominating all of them. The dogs found the food and cleared it, so that all the men saw was an empty bowl whose significance did not strike them. Torran used a battered enamel dish which might well have been dumped.

They called the Jack Russells and leashed them. Not tonight. But the questing noses told the men of the new family deep in the brambles and the dogs could easily get through. When it was time. Torran saw them in the moonlight, both big, both young, wearing jeans and leather jackets, with dark hair and sideburns and eyes that glinted with glee.

Vixen or woman, she thought. They would pursue either with as much dedication, caring not at all what happened to their victims, intent only on their own satisfaction. She waited for a long time before she dared climb down and make her way back to the cottage.

Jan, watching for her, hating her night-time prowling, felt anguish return at the sight of her white face and trembling body. He held her hand as she sat on the couch in the sitting-room, sick and shaking, not wanting to be alone. She would not tell him what had triggered memory, nor of her additional fear of more of the vicious letters. He had worries enough, without her adding to them.

He built the fire high, persuaded her to lie down, covered her with blankets and filled a hot-water bottle. He sat, pretending to read, while she lay staring at nothing, lost in a world of misery that she could not share.

The men were still on the hill when Ric woke and suckled again. His mother nursed the cubs against her. They were her first litter and the deep instincts that overrode everything else in her taught her to safeguard them against all danger. She listened, her body aware of the push and suck of the small mouths, a wild elation filling her.

Then came a sighing wind which brought her news of the dogs outside. She curled herself more tightly, her heart beating fast, ready to fight any intruder. The scent died away and she relaxed, knowing when the vibration of heavy footsteps stopped that the threat was gone for the time being.

She nuzzled each cub, savouring the small bodies, the seeking mouths, the small flattened ears. She licked the blind faces and was filled with a driving instinct to protect

57

them from harm. These were hers to bring to maturity, to teach all she knew. They would grow and learn from her as she had learnt when a cub.

She licked Ric's small head as he pulled at the biggest teat, the one between her hind legs. He was always first to find the best milk, pushing his brothers and sister roughly away. As he took more than they, he grew faster and daily became stronger.

There were more footsteps on the ground. The vixen's sensitive ears caught the sound and her body felt the tremor through the earth as the man walked. It was only Lyan, moving like a shadow, who had made a detour so that he could follow the intruders, wondering if he could find their van and report them, but she did not know that.

Elf knew that men meant death. She knew of the hunt and she knew of the cubs seized by terriers. Her two brothers had died. Her mate had been taken from her, and she knew that was due to humans. There had been the smell of humans all round the last place at which she found his scent. Her den was known to them and she had to find safety elsewhere.

She took Ric in her mouth, holding him by the scruff so that he dangled uncomfortably, often banging against the obstacles that she had to clear as she struggled up the hill. It was painful progress for both animals, as he was heavy. The way was hard, over tumbled sharp rocks that hurt her paws, through bracken and bramble, until she found a deep cleft which had sheltered her mother and herself and her sister when they were only a few weeks old. There was a tunnel at the back that drove deep into the ground.

The original den was in the hollow at the roots of a big, half-dead tree, nearly half a mile below. She took the cubs, one at a time, to the cleft, its mouth covered by bushes that fought towards the light. Here the trees were thickly planted, their trunks massive, their branches hiding the sun. She struggled through dense undergrowth, anxious to mask her trail. She crossed the stream, time and again, wading deep, keeping the cub high above the water. She was hungry and not as fast as she had been before the cubs were born.

It took her all night to move the four babies. Fear dominated her, as she knew that the smell of the recent birth would bring other predators. With the last in her mouth she trotted for almost a quarter of a mile through the brook to mask her trail, running as fast as she was able, milk filling her swinging teats so that they hampered her.

The moon was only a memory when she brought the little vixen to safety and lay, exhausted, while the cubs sucked, and she dozed, yet stayed alert, her ears listening, her nose questioning every breath of air. In spite of her fear she revelled in the sound and smell and feel of her babies, and was filled with a deep satisfaction beyond anything that she had ever experienced before.

Questing in the dawn, she caught a young rabbit, fed well, and returned to her family, always anxious lest weasel or stoat or rat found them. The rabbits were breeding fast and she had regained her skill and her speed. She did not need to add chicken to her diet and Jim waited, night after night, in vain, sure she would follow her mate's forays and begin on his hens. He planned to hunt for the litter himself and see that there were no cubs left to breed another year.

Torran, not realising that the vixen had moved her home, continued to leave food by the old earth. The bounty was welcomed by many creatures, so that its donor was at first unaware it had not reached its target. Elf knew better than to return to a dangerous lair, and was wary of Torran, having learnt that there was danger on the hill.

One evening, four weeks after the men had come with the Jack Russells, Ric, now able to see and to walk, although unsteadily, left the den when his mother slipped out to forage, and followed her trail, coming to a tiny clearing where he sat and stared astonished at the high moon above him, a slender curve of light, surrounded by pinpoint stars.

He had never seen trees before, nor the strange shapes of moving bushes. Too young to know fear, he watched them with intense curiosity, his small nose filled with overwhelming scents that meant nothing to him.

A wind ruffled his fur, and he tried to find the unseen presence, mystified by its touch. There were trees all round him, their branches sighing as they shivered. He was wild with young life and excited by his freedom. He dabbed at a grass stalk, watching, curious, as it bent beneath his questioning paw.

There were rabbit bones on the ground and he gnawed at one of them, using his mouth to answer his queries. Flavour and touch and sight and sense, and sound—that night he explored them all, whimpering as he pricked his paw on a thorn. He licked away the bead of blood, noting a new taste. The other cubs stayed in the den, as yet not as strong nor as inquisitive and adventurous as he.

Above him there was a soft sound on the air, and then a sudden whoosh as a passing owl saw him, sensing an easy meal. The vixen, on her way home with a rabbit in her mouth, dropped her prey when she heard the cub's startled cry as he was seized in sharp talons. She tore across the ground, leaping at the bird. Her snarling face and slashing paw caused him to falter and drop his victim. She snatched her wayward youngster and dived into sanctuary, nipping him and scolding him when at last they reached the den.

The gripping feet had torn the soft skin at the back of his neck, and he lay whimpering softly as his mother licked the wound and cuddled him against her, enticing him to suck.

She hated leaving the cubs, but she had to hunt and bring back food for them to eat, had to teach them how to hunt for themselves, had to carry her prey up the mountainside. The winter had been hard and many small beasts had died. Hawks and stoats and weasels all vied with her for bounty. She, like them, knew that the roads around the hill also provided food, and hunted for pheasants and hedgehogs that had died beneath racing wheels. Nothing was ever wasted. The crows and magpies watched and waited too. She brought home the greater part of her catch and half-starved herself for her cubs.

The men found her one dark night on the hillside. The questing dogs raced at her, snapping and snarling, dashing in to bite and darting out again, avoiding her snapping jaws.

She faced her tormentors, inflicting wounds herself, but she was weakened by her search for food for her litter. It took only minutes for the dogs to end her life. They were used to rat-catching and worked as a team, one flying in while the other barked and snapped and distracted his quarry.

Dawn came as the vixen died. She was well away from her den, and the men had no time to hunt now. They needed to be away before people were moving on Staghill, having no desire to be found and unaware that they had been seen by two pairs of eyes.

Lyan saw them leave. Torran had not been out that night, but the Colonel, also sleepless, had been sitting at his bedroom window, which he opened wide to take away the smell of forbidden tobacco smoke. He saw the men as they walked back to their van, but was unaware that they had brought tragedy to the foxes.

The cubs could wait for another foray. The two men and the dogs had had fun, though they would have regarded it as more successful if the vixen had not been so weak and had given the dogs a better fight before they killed her.

There would be more pleasure to come when they returned for the cubs. Waiting would add savour to the hunt. The terriers needed prey that would try at least to stand up for itself. They thought that the dog fox would feed them, unaware that he too was dead.

High above them the cubs listened in vain for their mother to return and whimpered with hunger.

Torran found the torn body of the vixen and was devastated. Lyan had found it first and was waiting for her. Silver, smelling death, hid himself well away from the man.

She looked up as Lyan detached himself from the shadows.

'It's only me,' he said softly, knowing she would be alarmed if she heard him and did not see him.

She stared at the mutilated vixen. She stroked her soft fur.

'She'd done no harm. Who'd do such a thing when she's in full milk? What'll happen to the cubs? They'll starve to death. I don't even know where she's hidden them.'

'Too well, maybe,' Lyan said. The thought had been worrying him too. He felt a strong desire for revenge but did not know how to wreak it. He was not sure who was responsible for the carnage, but suspected the men and their dogs. This was no swift shooting.

'She's never been near the food I put out for her. I saw the badgers take it twice. Do you think she's been after Jim's chickens?'

'Jim doesn't bring dogs,' Lyan said and promptly regretted the words, seeing the flash of fear as she recalled the previous visit of the men with their terriers, and knowing that she now had an added worry. The thought appalled her. She thought she had found peace but that had gone. Nowhere in the world was safe.

Panic, which had once been a constant her life, but had slowly faded, now returned, so that she hid herself by day and was wary in the woods, returning home fast as soon as Silver vanished, not knowing that it was only Lyan, watching over her safety, himself roused to extreme anxiety since the intruders had come.

She did not wait to find out who was there, and for a while their meetings ceased. Death had brought an extra wariness to Silver, and at times he warned her when no one was near, having heard voices rising from the village on still air.

Elf joined Blacktip in the little cemetery at the end of the garden. Torran needed to overcome her terror and find the cubs before the men came back. Unless she could rescue them, they were doomed. If the dogs did not kill them they would starve. They were much too small to hunt successfully for themselves.

That evening the Colonel had another letter to show to Lyan. Jan had found it with his mail. He was unaware of the others that Torran had found, pinned to the door at night so that she would see them on her return.

DEATH HAS COME TO STAGHILL. YOU COULD FOLLOW THE BEASTS. BEWARE!

'Do you think this is part of a campaign to drive them away?' he asked Lyan. 'Jan is very concerned. So far he's been able to keep them from Torran but he's afraid she might open one, if he doesn't get the mail himself.'

'Tell him I'll pick it up with ours on my way to school and I'll go down for it on Saturdays,' Lyan said. The two mailboxes were at the foot of the hill, to save the postmen a long journey on foot.

He thought for a minute.

'The men I saw aren't local. Jim Cartwright killed the dog fox: he's boasted about it in the pub. Dogs killed the vixen and the men had terriers with them. No one in the village has Jack Russells. Someone knows about the

63

death of the foxes, but I wouldn't think that outsiders would write such letters. I don't see any point.'

'Have you had experience of them?'

'They're very hard to trace, unless we can actually see someone putting one in the mailbox. There might be fingerprints, but whose? We can only trace those if they are on record.' He had unconsciously returned to his old role in life. 'It looks like an ordinary ballpoint pen and the notebooks the paper's torn from are in every news-agent and schoolroom.'

'This time, we tell the police. Torran's distraught and intent on finding the cubs. Suppose the men catch her on the hill by herself? Perhaps we could find them. I don't know how, unless maybe Quint and Sapphire could nose them out. They'll be about five weeks old, I'd guess. Jan said the vixen had had the cubs when he saw her about a month back. Too young to hunt for themselves.'

There had been no sign of Elf since the men's first visit and Lyan had no idea where she had hidden her litter. He did not know where to start searching. That night Torran roamed through the woods, stopping often to listen for tell-tale cries. The cubs would be suffering from extreme hunger and calling to their mother.

Lyan felt a desperate pity as he watched her. She glimpsed him, but did not want to talk. She reminded him of a neighbour's cat whose kittens had been destroyed just after they were born. The little animal had hunted through the gardens, calling desperately, looking under bushes, in the crevices of trees, her cries haunting him.

High on the hill, too far away to be heard, the cubs' continual cries were weakening. There were other unwel-come listeners, biding their time, knowing that here was easy prey, and that soon the cubs would be too weak to resist.

The predators gathered.

Six

The central part of Lynsom Green had been unchanged for centuries, the straggle of old cottages, each with its own flower-filled garden, hiding the small new development of council houses and a tiny bungalow estate.

Lyan found it extraordinary after the busy city in which he had lived and worked. It was a place that seemed to have dropped out of time and to be thirty years behind the rest of the world. Its crimes were small crimes, and here people walked the streets at night, never dreaming of danger. Cottage doors remained unlocked by day.

Everyone left the money for the milk on the doorstep and Lyan, talking to the school Head in his first weeks there, had expressed surprise.

'Our chief problem is Joe McToul,' she said. 'Daft as a brush, that one, with no more wits than a little boy of four and him nearly fifty. No danger in him, mind, but if you find things go missing, just ask Tom or Madge, nicely. It's usually Joe.'

Seeing Lyan's bemused expression she laughed.

'We're used to him. Just don't say you need something, like a bicycle or new coat, in his hearing: he'll go and find you one and bring it, like a dog that's bringing his ball back with his tail wagging. Means no harm. He just can't understand, that's all. Property, to him, is communal. He'll quite happily give you his most precious possession if you admire it.'

The village had an amazing tolerance of its own; very little indeed for those it deemed outsiders, and deep hatred of the two couples who had bought holiday homes and came only at weekends, finding that they were totally ignored, especially as they brought their own supplies and did not patronise the village shop.

Lyan still felt an alien, as strange to them as if he had come from Mars, and at times as unable to understand their motivation. It had been months before he summoned enough courage to venture into the Dog and Duck for a frugal half-pint of bitter.

He rarely repeated the experience. Unless the Colonel was there he was ignored, but after seeing the second anonymous letter he thought perhaps he might find a clue to the writer if he listened to the gossip.

The place was crowded. Nobody greeted him, nobody smiled at him. Two of the children's fathers nodded to him. He was constantly aware of the eyes that slid away in embarrassment when they saw his scarred face.

An unusually handsome man before the shooting, he felt deformed. A bullet anywhere else would have been endurable; no one would have seen the after-effects. But he had a daily reminder, and could not grow a beard as the plastic surgeon had replaced the injured tissue with hairless skin. He hated his mirror, but needed it to comb the thick thatch of hair that threatened to curl if it were not cut in time.

The Dog and Duck was a shooting man's haven—prints on the wall of hunters with spaniels, or flights of pheasants, or ducks on an estuary. The mere sight of the pictured guns brought back fear.

He crossed to the far side of the room, moving like a cat around the extreme edge, hiding the right side of his face and feeling conspicuous.

Effie Green was surrounded by an eager group, anxious to hear the snippets of gossip that she had painstakingly collected during the week. They lost nothing in telling as what Effie didn't know was made up by her vivid imagination. Her audience listened avidly.

She had a genius for misunderstanding that often led her into difficulties. She meant well, people said, with weary sighs, as they had when she called the police who broke into Grebe Cottage. The couple who lived there had gone out in the dark and forgotten to pull back the curtains. Effie was convinced they were both dead in bed, gassed by fumes. They saw nothing kind in her intention or in her worries about them.

A lonely woman, she needed occupation, which the village did not provide. In her more sober moments she knew she would be wiser to think before she spoke.

'A new young vet,' Effie said now. 'Very young. Old Mac's past it.'

Tonight she was dressed in one of her more extravagant outfits, a shapeless purple smock covered by a bright emerald waistcoat. A string of brown wooden beads hung almost to waist-level. Her chestnut hair, which the rest of the village suspected owed its colour to Emmie Robins, who carried on her business in her own back room, was tied with a scarlet ribbon. The outfit was not improved by white ankle socks and trainers.

Lyan, leaning against the wall, listened in some amusement. Mary Dunnet, the landlady of the Dog and Duck, was busy speculating on the fact that with a young man, not village bred, no girl would be safe and they would need to watch their daughters. He knew very well that the girls in question were as likely to fall victim to the village lads as to any outsider. Lynsom Green did not specialise in saints.

Effie's shrill voice carried even above the juke box din.

'This new vet's too young and I won't be taking my boy to him,' she said, referring to her grossly overweight and bad-tempered ginger tom, who spent most of his time sitting on the window-sill, gibbering at birds he could never catch even if he tried. Effie had never married.

'There's too many coming in. The Colonel and those foreigners he brought. Refugees, he said. From Bosnia or somewhere, I suppose. Her grandfather, he says. They don't even look alike.'

Lyan stifled a snorting laugh, glad that Torran did not resemble her neat grey-bearded grandfather. Effie, becoming garrulous thanks to her third glass of white wine, which she was sure was a tonic and not an intoxicating drink, was off again like a hound picking up a fresh trail. 'And there's the new schoolmaster too.'

New, Lyan thought, having been there now for over two years, and wondering at the intolerance of the villagers. He knew they had not wanted him. It should have been their Jennie Leigh who became assistant at the little village school, but Jennie was away to Shrewsbury in disgrace, nobody knowing the father of her baby boy and she not telling.

'An ill-favoured man,' Mary Dunnet said, unaware that the subject of their gossip stood only a few yards away, hidden by others between him and the little group. It was her night off and Sally Dene was serving at the bar, tossing her curls and her smiles alike at the men and ignoring the women. She had barely noticed the schoolmaster when she served him, being intent on flirting with Jack Emery who sold insurance and had a good job in Pyneton, as well as a smart fast car.

Mary was still talking.

'One side of his face so scarred it's not easy to look at. He comes from Liverpool. You know what goes on there.'

'Gangs with razors, and drugs and glue-sniffing,' said Tom McToul. Cities were terrible places. You saw it all the time on the television. No one was safe walking there at night, nor, at times, by day. Gun battles and murders. They all knew that.

'And what's a man his age doing without a wife? You don't think . . . ? He's with the children, too.'

68

Lyan was unprepared for the sudden burst of fury that possessed him, to be succeeded even more terrifyingly by the black despair that he hoped had gone for ever. He remembered the odd looks he received from the postmistress when he went to the shop.

He nerved himself. He had promised himself he would listen and try to find out what motivated the villagers, and he regarded a promise as sacred, to be fulfilled at all costs if humanly possible. He could not run away now, no matter how he felt, even though nobody but he would know of his failure.

There was a little bench with a high back where he could sit unseen and still overhear. He took his beer and slipped into its shelter.

Donald Trent, the vicar, had been standing behind the group and seen Lyan. He tried to pluck up his courage to remonstrate with Effie and Mary whose tongues at times caused him immense problems.

There was the terrible week when the charity money from the church bazaar had disappeared. All four hundred pounds of it, safe, Donald thought, in the vicarage study. Who would look for cash in a tin labelled 'Teatime Assortment'? He had panicked and reported its loss, afraid he might be thought to have been indulging in theft himself.

He did not discover until a week later that his wife, who had gone away to care for her mother after an operation, had been worried by having so much money in the house and had taken it to the bank and forgotten to tell him.

She only learned of his misery when she returned home to find him distraught. Meanwhile Effie had accused three members of the church in turn. They all now attended service in the next village, having vowed never to darken his doors again.

Remembering, he knew he had to break into the conversation. Idle gossip caused too much trouble and unhappiness. He knew why Lyan's face was scarred and had heard his unhappy history.

'The Colonel tells me Lyan Grant was injured on duty, by a bank robber. He was a policeman,' he said.

'The Colonel now . . .' said Mary, sniffing, undaunted. 'Two men living together . . .' She needed to say no more. Her audience knew exactly what she meant. Lyan, trapped in his seat, not wishing to reveal himself after what had been said, listened in mounting anger and horror.

Perhaps for both their sakes he should leave the Place, but he enjoyed living there. He was becoming oversensitive. People always gossiped and much of what they said was lies.

'The schoolmaster has his own flat there,' Effie said, overtaken by a sudden desire to be fair. Funny how your tongue ran away with you after a few glasses of wine, she thought, guilt needling. 'Little Mark Luton called one day because he'd forgotten to take his homework to school. Full of big photographs of wild animals, Mark said. Right at the top of the house.'

The group chatted on, tossing ideas from one to another, happily unaware that they had an eavesdrooper. What would happen to the Big House when he died? Would he leave it to some outsider, the schoolmaster perhaps, or would it be sold and pulled down for development? Speculation was rife though the Colonel showed no sign of ill health or frailty.

'Soon be nobody left in the village who belongs,' Tom McToul said.

Tom was an awkward neighbour, being convinced that the world was due to end every January 1st. He was undeterred by the fact that so far some twenty years had passed without such an event, since he was informed of its imminence by a strange God who sometimes spoke to him in his dreams.

He helped the Colonel on occasion, making his stints

in the woods and the garden seem a tremendous favour, although he had no other work. The Colonel had learnt to close his ears to tales of doom and disaster.

The vicar and Tom frequently came almost to blows, although neither was easily roused to anger. Tom knew better than the clergyman just what should be preached in church and had no time for a merciful deity.

A vicar with a temper is an insult to God, Donald's wife told him, and he knelt in the gloomy church and prayed for self-control and forgiveness, being of a nature that in other times would have worn hair shirts and used whips to flagellate himself.

Effie ran most of the village activities. She was President of the Women's Institute, and Chairman of the Mothers' Union. Mary had founded a Moral Watch Committee that was the bane of the vicar's life. Effie, not to be outdone, started a Neighbourhood Watch, driving Matt Grey, the village policeman, to wish her anywhere but on his patch.

'Jan Ardan visits the Colonel. Calls in often,' Tom said, pursuing another obsession. 'Plotting, I reckon.'

'Someone should report them.' Mary was not at all sure what they would report or whom they would tell.

'Was he really in the army?' Tom asked. 'Suppose those two are enemy spies, and they're planning to blow us all up?'

Lyan nearly choked on his beer. He had a sudden vision of Jan and the Colonel with their heads together over the fishing flies that Jan made so deftly. Had they been seen through a window and their actions misinterpreted, or was it just another of Tom's wild ideas, on no evidence at all?

The vicar sighed, wondering when prejudice would cease.

'He says she's his granddaughter.' Mary's small dark eyes sparked with malice, her tone showing very well how she interpreted that.

71

'Who's to know? No better than a witch with her brews and the beasts she takes in,' Tom said. He liked to be part of the Friday gossip group, collecting information as a crow collected bright baubles if it got half a chance.

Effie, who used herbs herself, was about to interrupt, but Tom gave her no opportunity. Aware that he was only tolerated, and rarely listened to, especially when he tried to prepare everyone for the Day of Doom, he had a titbit of his own to offer and was determined that they should take notice. They might mock at Doomsday, but nobody in Lynsom Green would mock at this.

'The white stag's back.'

There was a sudden silence. As far as they were concerned the white stag meant disaster, and its coming to the woods was a rare event. Nobody realised that the wary beast, always there, was seldom seen.

'Who saw it?' The vicar hated the village stories. They frightened the more timid children and gave them nightmares.

'I saw it,' Tom said. 'Walking along behind the Ardan woman. Following her like a dog, it was. Doomed, she is, I reckon, in the next few months. Won't even last to January 1st.'

He made it sound as if that was to be a great occasion, perhaps as exciting as the annual fair, or the winter pantomime that was put on faithfully by the drama group. The vicar wondered why it would be a disaster to die before the day the world ended, which presumably was not going to be a pleasant occasion for anyone.

Sighing, he went outside. Lyan took advantage of a sudden influx of customers to slip out too, and joined him. The village street straggled towards the green and the slim-spired church stood sentinel beyond a lych-gate that Americans came to photograph, exclaiming at its quaintness. It was half-hidden in darkness, the scattered street lamps revealing little.

They stood together, staring at the post office window, which was plastered with cards offering kittens free to good homes, or puppies for sale.

'They're like children. They don't mean half they say,' the vicar said, aware that the schoolmaster must have heard the whole conversation. 'Mary's an odd woman with a spiteful tongue. I suspect Effie's afraid to disagree, but she's kindness itself when anyone's in trouble.'

Lyan, knowing that the vicar hated to think ill of anyone, very much doubted that. A desire to know more, and to meddle, he thought.

'People are the same the world over. Join a golf club, a dog club, a tennis club, a youth club . . . How long before you're accepted and not ignored, or worse, completely ostracised?'

He sketched a brief salute before leaving Donald to make his way home, pondering on his parish. Should his Sunday sermon deal with prejudice and ask for tolerance? Might as well tell Jim Cartwright's very pregnant sow not to farrow, he thought wearily as he turned into the little gravelled drive that led to his front door.

And there was another problem. Jim was a violent man, and his temper was growing worse as his farm plunged into ever more difficulty. His wife had visited the vicarage in tears only three days before, and Donald had no idea how to help her. Her husband was becoming paranoid. Every new edict from the Ministry or from Brussels seemed angled at him deliberately to cut his income to starvation level. Nobody else suffered as he did.

His farm was the biggest in the district, some of the fields rising to meet the woods on Staghill. Jim was village born and village bred, and ignorant.

Life was not made easier by his conviction that if an animal died it was because of ill-luck brought to the village by the Ardan woman. He was obsessed and, worse, was influencing Lucy, who spent her time in running battle with her mother. The marriage now was bereft of affection and if Alison had seen another way of living she would have left Jim long ago. As it was, the farm owed what prosperity it had to her and Will and she was not depriving her son of his inheritance.

'There's no arguing with him,' she had told Donald Trent wearily. 'He's beyond sense.'

Lyan had learnt little except that all incomers were disliked and distrusted. Any one of those in Effie's group might have written the letters, but which of them knew of the death of the vixen? Jim had bragged in the Dog and Duck about his killing of the dog fox. There was no mystery about that.

*　　*　　*

The Colonel had gone to bed. Lyan, finding his room as unwelcoming as the villagers themselves, took his night-glasses and went out into the darkness. The vixen had been dead for four days; the cubs must be starving. He wondered how long it would take them to die. Were they old enough to dig around for grubs in the ground and wise enough to eat roots and grasses? He had no idea.

He climbed through the memories of last year's bracken, feeling the wind on his face, and, surrounded by the noises of the night, began at last to relax.

He felt awkward and ill at ease, having been reminded too forcefully of his disfigurement. He needed solitude. Well hidden, he watched Torran as she searched the hill, listening for the desperate sounds of hungry cubs. She paused as the old badger boar followed his well-trodden trail down the hill towards the stream and stopped to drink, his lapping noisy. He was used to her presence and ignored her.

His mate was safe underground with her own cubs. He foraged through the bushes, without caution. The white stag, cuddled in a depression in the bracken, heard him and moved away, meeting Torran. He greeted her, nosing her, and Lyan wished he had brought his camera. If only he could show the secret film he was making. There were scenes that even he found hard to believe although he had recorded them.

Moonlight dappled the ground and it was easy to imagine that Silver indeed was a ghost creature as he paced silently, his coat gleaming, a visitor from some other realm.

The badger crossed their path and the stag bounded into the darkness beneath the trees and was gone. Torran turned to watch the big boar blunder through the undergrowth. If the men who had killed the vixen discovered there were badgers too, there would be little peace. She needed to protect them. But how? Her fears for the animals overcame her own panic.

Lyan thought of the intruders too, knowing they would persecute the badgers with as much dedication as they would the cubs, coming again and again until there were none left. What would put off such men?

He watched until the grey dawn brightened to the colours of day and Torran, giving up her futile search, went wearily into the cottage, knowing that time was short and wondering how much longer the cubs could survive. She approached the door with dread, but there was no message today.

At the back of the cleft on the hill the cubs whimpered still more forlornly for the mother who had deserted them. The pathetic cries grew in strength as hunger goaded them, and their small bodies ached for food.

Seven

The descendants of the gamekeeper's cats laired high on Staghill, finding shelter in abandoned dens. The original pair had run off to live in the wild more than fifteen years ago. Their offspring, without human contact, were as wary as any true wild cat and had learnt skill, speed and cunning.

One of them, a pretty animal, her dense coat mottled black and ginger and white, had survived to almost eighteen months old because she was fast, she was wily and she was an adept hunter. Few mice or rats survived her onslaught.

She had lost her first litter, born when she was only six months old, to the biggest tom cat who killed any that he found. She fared no better with her second litter, which was killed soon after birth by the same marauding tom. Too many cats on the hill would lack prey, and the stock would starve. Nature operated her own controls.

For her third litter she chose a tiny hollowed-out rock, well away from the other cats, inside a cave, and gloried in her three new kits, barely leaving them until they were almost a week old and she was desperate for food.

She had chosen unwisely, as there was little for her to catch and kill close to the nest and she had to wander. There were others with families near her, among them an unusually large weasel, who had caught the birth scent and monitored her hiding-place, knowing the litter was still vulnerable.

The kittens, abandoned and hungry as their mother was hunting, whimpered, and the watcher knew that they were alone. Every time the cat went out for food, another kitten disappeared.

By the time they were nine days old, not one was left and she was heavy in milk, deep in discomfort and bereft. She haunted the hill, searching in vain for her lost litter, and heard the cubs crying. She came upon them, at the mouth of the cleft, too weak to stray far from their base.

As she approached, hidden in the undergrowth, a sparrowhawk dived. The cat leaped at him, fur fluffed and claws raking, spitting and snarling her defiance, so that he changed his mind and soared again, leaving the cubs safe for the present. She had lost her own young and she needed a family desperately. The hunger wails triggered every instinct she had and there was an instant adoption.

She went to them, licking each, implanting her scent on them, and they, smelling milk, began to suckle, although they were ready for weaning. When they had fed she led them back into the safety of the cleft and curled herself around them, licking them over and over, holding Ric, who complained bitterly, with a firm paw. She slept, comforted, and woke and licked them again, cleaning eyes and ears and noses, cleaning their small bodies, cleaning under their tails, and when she had done startled them by her loud, happy purr.

The cries ceased, and when they slept the little cat went hunting, bringing back a baby rabbit, part of which she ate. The rest she left for the cubs. Within a week the litter was hers and she their mother. They watched for her, running to greet her, small brushes waving. They nosed her, begging for food. Their tiny prick-eared faces peered out of the undergrowth, eager for her return and the bounty that she brought them.

Her thwarted instincts guided her, so that they learned to play with her twitching tail, pouncing with ever more accuracy as they grew. She twisted it away from them, teasing them, provoking them to bigger bounds, so that

77

small muscles hardened and small skills were perfected.

She brought half-dead mice and rats to help them learn, and grew thin and shabby-coated as she struggled to satisfy the ever-growing appetites.

Her adopted cubs gave her immense satisfaction. She spent hours grooming them, in spite of vigorous protests, holding them down with a paw, exerting all her effort as they were now growing strong. The cleft had been well chosen, far away from intruders, and nobody thought of looking there.

Lyan and Torran gave up their search, sure the cubs had succumbed to starvation or been taken by hawk or stoat or weasel.

It was easy to copy their new mother, as they were naturally catlike, moving lightly like kittens rather than pups. Ric chased the shaking grass-heads, leaped at a feather blowing in the wind, caught it, and carried it everywhere, his special trophy. Originally white, from a magpie's wing, it was soon battered and bent and filthy, but he would not part with it. His two brothers and his sister tried to take it from him, but that was never allowed and he guarded it jealously, snarling at them if they came too near.

They did not challenge. He had always taken the largest share of the milk and also managed to grab more bounty than they from his foster-mother's kills. He grew fast into a small adventurous animal, seeking to explore beyond the safety of the nest.

The cat led the cubs out at night, intent on teaching them to hunt. They followed her, an unlikely little procession. She turned often to make sure they were safe, and taught them how to react at a footstep on the ground, or a rustle in the bushes, or the shadow cast in a moonlit glade by the softly flying owl.

She had learnt well and knew that wise animals lay stiller than the stones around them. Foolish animals ran, triggering a chase. Freeze, she told the cubs. Hide from the hunting hawk. Hide from the flying owl. Hide from the beasts that seek to end your lives. Her body gave them signals and they learned that if they did not obey her she punished them, with nipping teeth and slapping paw, and sometimes unsheathed claws.

Ric had memories of his first adventure. There was a scar on his neck, under the fur, which would never go. He crouched at once when the owl flew overhead, hiding himself in the shivering grass, or under the bushes. He learned to avoid the sharp prickles of the furze when he backed unwarily into a bush as a badger prowled by, startling all of them.

When the moon was high the cat brought the cubs out into the open where they played, wrestling with one another, rolling over, their ears flattened as they indulged in mock fights. Small mouths snarled, and small bodies grew supple as they exercised.

Ric was more interested in exploring than in his brothers and sister. The cat was for ever shepherding him back, chivvying him, slapping him, hissing at him, trying to teach him to be wary, to listen, to watch. At first she carried him by the scruff, dragging him along, determined to keep him safe, but he was soon too heavy for her.

His wonderful new world enchanted him. There was so much to discover, so much to remember. He listened to the rustles in the bushes. They might be caused by a mouse running over dead leaves, or a bird foraging for insects.

One Friday evening Lyan, intent on walking and on the peace of the hill, caught a glimpse of movement and focused his binoculars.

He did not believe what he saw. The little cat was stretched out at ease far above him, the fox cubs cuddled round her, one lying with his head on her flank, another tucked beneath her chin. Ric was just beyond her, stretched full length, his thick brush beneath her neck.

79

The fourth cub was tucked between her legs. They were nearly as big as their unlikely foster-mother.

'The cubs are safe,' he told the Colonel that evening as they ate. It had been one of the worst weeks he had had so far, as two of the children in his class, emboldened by their new friendship, were posing problems. Alone, they were mischievous and unpleasantly imaginative. Together, they seemed to be almost lethal. Neither he nor his colleague had any idea how to deal with them. The cubs were a welcome distraction. 'They seem to have been adopted by one of the wild cats.'

'That's astonishing.' The Colonel was briefly distracted from his own thoughts. 'I wonder how many there are.' He was thoughtful. 'I've seen at least seven different animals since I came to live here, but you never catch more than a glimpse. They're wild as any fox.'

'You'd think someone would have taken them in when they first took to the hill.' Lyan could not bear the thought of any animal suffering from neglect, and two well-loved cats must have found life without shelter or warmth extremely tough after living in the cottage.

'Apparently Cousin Stephanie tried, but had to give up as they refused ever to come indoors. She fed them, but they resisted all attempts at domestication, and as she became older she forgot them, and much else besides.'

He stared out of the window. Heavy clouds had hidden the sun and rain threatened.

'Matt says that the poachers' van has been seen again in the clearing at the foot of the hill. It was empty and nobody saw the men, or the dogs. He kept watch but had to go to a road accident. Someone knocked a cyclist down.'

He was not eating his food, but toying with it, moving it aimlessly around the plate. Dorothy Burton had excelled herself, cooking a casserole that had featured the night before in one of the television series. It tasted wonderful.

Lyan watched with disquiet, wondering if the Colonel were unwell and refusing to admit the fact.

'Sapphire's ill,' the older man said, giving up any attempt to eat. 'I took her to Mac this afternoon. He called in the new youngster for a consultation. She's picked up poison—strychnine, he thinks. Maybe not a full dose, but he isn't sure she'll live. He's working on her. The convulsions were terrifying. I don't see how she can survive.'

The dogs were always under the table when the men were eating, so that Lyan had not noticed her absence, and had not realised that Quint, distraught by the loss of his companion, was sitting beside the Colonel, doing his best to remain unnoticed, not realising that his solid body, pressed against his master's leg, betrayed his presence.

The Colonel had no desire to shift him. The dog could not understand why his companion was missing. Roger couldn't bear to think of life without her and her endearing ways.

'How did she get it?' Lyan asked, extremely disturbed by the news, and wondering if it had any connection with the anonymous letters. Poisoned bait might be found by any animal, by the cubs and the cat, by any of the local pets. 'Have you told Jan?'

'I rang and warned him. I think she found it near their cottage. She was foraging in the undergrowth. It could have been meant for one of their animals. Or maybe there was a carcass with poison in it laid for the foxes, and crows have been at it and taken pieces and dropped them. It could be everywhere. Mac's warning the villagers to keep away and make sure their dogs are leashed when they are out.'

'Jim Cartwright?'

'He's capable of it. He hates the foxes and he's anything but rational these days. I'd be surprised if his wife would let him, though. She still has some control over what he does and she hates poison. Won't even have it down for the rats. Says the cats will catch them and there's no need.

'Have you time to talk?' he asked abruptly as Lyan turned towards the staircase, intending to spend the evening in his own quarters marking the children's essays. He never stayed long with his landlord after their evening meal, unless invited.

The log fire in the study blazed brightly. They ate their meals there, preferring the occasional table to the formal state of the dining-room. Quint walked over and dropped to the rug in front of it, his eyes forlorn. He had spent the afternoon looking for Sapphire in every cranny in the house, and then hunted the garden.

He was finally convinced that she had vanished. The Colonel suspected that if he were free he would search the hill, hoping desperately to pick up her trail. Now he mourned for her, sure she would never return.

'He won't even touch his food.'

The Colonel stooped and put down the remnants of his own meal in the dog's bowl. Quint walked over and looked at it, his ears flat on his head. He moved as if life were a burden. He gave a few tentative licks and then returned to the hearthrug where he dropped with a deep sigh and put his nose on his master's foot, looking up at him, his eyes asking why he was alone.

The Colonel stretched his legs out to the blaze and leaned back in his chair.

'I thought that retiring here would be pleasant,' he said. 'In the last few weeks something seems to have stirred the whole village to show its hatred. Someone's trying to drive us away. Me, the Ardans, maybe you.'

'Would you go?'

'This is my home now. Why should I leave it? No one wanted it any more than they wanted the derelict game-keeper's cottage. If the Ardans hadn't worked on it, it would be a ruin by now.'

Lyan was aware of a feeling of great unease. He looked

up at the hill, at the wooded buttresses, at the streaked clouds that hung above it, and thought of the many beasts that lived there, all at risk.

He was startled out of his reverie by the ringing phone. The Colonel stared at it as if afraid of the message it would bring.

'Mac said he'd ring about now. If Sapphire's dead . . .'

Lyan looked at the instrument, willing it to bring good news. If the bitch died then Staghill was doomed and nobody was safe. If she survived, so too would the hill and the beasts he had come to love.

Please God, he said inside his head as the Colonel picked up the receiver. As a little boy he had often made pacts with whatever deity was there. Please let everything be all right and I'll be good for ever. He had a memory of his small desperate self trying to seek absolution for some childish misdeed. It had been a talisman when life was rough. He chided himself for his reversion but the thought persisted.

Outside the window the sun died among streaked red clouds, and the wind rustled the trees. A branch tapped eerily against the window, the effect heightened by the soft, low hooting of a distant owl and a mournful reply from the woods beyond.

Eight

It seemed a long time before the Colonel put the receiver down. He walked across to the fireplace, staring sombrely at the bowl of potpourri that his housekeeper had amazed him by giving him for his birthday. The cloying scent filled the room and he wondered if she hated the smell of men and drowned it in this way.

'He thinks she has a chance. We won't know for certain till tomorrow. If she survives tonight . . .'

Lyan looked down at Quint who lay with both marrow bones, ignored, by his front paws. He nosed them, as if there might be some lingering memory of Sapphire to comfort him. When the Colonel whistled he stretched himself and walked over slowly, sitting in front of the men, his brown eyes mournful. He put up his paw to his master, who took it and held it as if not quite knowing what to do next. The Colonel offered him his bone. He looked at it without interest and lay down with a deep sigh.

Lyan picked up the bones and put them out of reach and out of sight on top of the high bookcase. Roger took his empty pipe, holding it as if it were a talisman that would bring comfort. He sighed, putting it back, then changed his mind and sucked it, hoping for a faint tease of tobacco.

'It's not very good news,' he said at last. 'It could have affected her brain; or weakened her so much that any minor illness will see her off; or damaged her kidneys or liver. Mac used a stomach pump. He's given her an anaesthetic, which will stop the convulsions. She's still alive, but he had another patient with the same symptoms:

one of the Cartwright cats. If it was Jim, then his act has rebounded, as the cat's dead.'

That was no comfort at all.

'Mac says to ring in the morning.'

Lyan wished it were not the weekend. He could have lost himself in his teaching. The Colonel, sitting stroking Quint, sighed.

Sapphire was his sanity, his pleasure, his delight. He loved Quint but the dog was less affectionate towards humans than the bitch, who had bonded to her master from the moment they met and hated him out of her sight.

Sapphire was also the focus of Quint's life. Without her he was distraught, having relied on her not only for company but for guidance. She had mothered him as a pup and he was totally lost without her.

The Colonel had bought the bitch soon after he moved to his new home and had the right environment for an active dog. It had been a longstanding promise to himself that, if he ever lived in a suitable place, he would reward himself with a German Shepherd. He had not expected that wish to come true. The dogs forced him to remember his good fortune and the unregretted little flat that had been his first home after retirement.

'Will I take him to the kitchen now?' Mrs Burton asked, startling both men who had been lost in their own thoughts, and had not noticed her come in with the coffee tray.

Lyan masked a grin as the Colonel hastily put his pipe back on the mantelpiece, covering the action by poking the fire in the hope that the housekeeper had not noticed.

'He's staying with me tonight. He's lost without Sapphire.'

'He'll not sleep in your room! Dogs should never be in bedrooms. It's bad enough having them in the house. The dirty beasts should have kennels.'

The Colonel looked at her, irritated, feeling that there were times when she forgot her place.

'He sleeps where I choose. I'm not leaving him on his own.' Quint was watching him, his head on one side as if trying to understand what was being said. One ear moved, trying to trap the sound, seeking comfort from the voice.

Dorothy Burton seemed to have no desire to leave the room. There was a bright flush on her cheeks, but her eyes were downcast, hiding anger. The dogs, with their muddy paws and shed hairs, added immeasurably to her work and nobody could call the two men either thoughtful or tidy. She chose to ignore the fact that Lyan kept his own room clean and she only changed the sheets once a week and gave it what she called a thorough do, knowing men were incapable of paying attention to their surroundings.

She irritated him by tidying up the books on his desk, which were in deliberate piles: those he had corrected; those he had corrected but wished to look at again as they needed more thought about the children's capability of learning; and those as yet uncorrected. Since the three piles were always neat he could not understand her obsession. She hated newspapers and magazines as well, lying around cluttering up the place.

She was restless, needing the security of absolute tidiness. She looked at the mantelpiece and aligned the six china owls so that they stood in a precise row. She removed the pipe, handling it with disgust, and put it in the pristine ashtray on a side table.

She turned towards the photograph, once more prominent on top of the desk, but saw the Colonel's expression, as if he dared her to move it, and changed her mind. One of his women, she supposed. She often wondered about it, but had never dared to ask. She was sure both men had a chequered history. All men did.

To make her point she took the newspaper and refolded it more neatly, putting it down on the windowsill, at right angles to the edge. Even there it seemed out of place and she moved it again to another side table. The two men watched her, puzzled. She seemed unusually on edge.

Her thoughts were seething. The day had not gone as she wished. The need to take Sapphire to the vet had meant that the evening meal was late, cutting into her free time.

She ought to be grateful to Roger Manton for taking her away from the squalid bedsitting-room, but she wasn't. She resented her need, she resented him, and she was old, over sixty. She yearned for retirement and a life of her own choosing. The men would never understand. She masked her feelings and kept her eyes lowered so that they would not see the flash of anger, or the feelings of dislike or contempt.

She dreamed of a little house when her work was done and she sat alone in the two rooms that, though giving her ample accommodation, were part of someone else's home. Nothing in them was hers except for the ornaments and pictures. Her married life had been spent in army quarters and then, when Ted died, there was only the squalid room from which the Colonel had rescued her. It was such a small pension . . .

Here, there was always too much to do. Jan Ardan called at inconvenient hours, delaying her work because she could not clean around him. She hated the old house, its immense size and the big ugly furniture that was heavy to move. She liked everything in a precise place, set neatly against the walls.

The Colonel liked the settee in the big sitting-room at an angle, as otherwise it masked the radiator and absorbed heat that should have gone into the room. She put it straight. The room when she had finished her daily work reminded him of the waiting area in a doctor's or a solicitor's premises. He sometimes thought they were engaged in a covert running battle that nobody else noticed.

Gardens should be made up of neat lines of tidy plants whose heads were cut off before they died or straggled. Not, like this one, a wild abundance of every flower under the sun, in any sort of order. That was not her province and even on the finest summer day she stayed indoors.

Tom McToul was responsible for its appearance. He had been delighted when the Colonel offered him the chance to plan as he liked. He loved the old-fashioned cottage gardens and Roger gave him his head. Tom had nothing but a back yard. The Colonel did not know that Madge McToul grew geraniums in pots, set neatly round the area. Tom loathed geraniums and neat flowerbeds.

Mrs Burton loathed Tom McToul, especially if Joe came with him. She kept the men outside for the mid-morning and afternoon drinks the Colonel insisted she gave them, not allowing them into the kitchen, even if it rained. They brought their own food.

She disliked her work more daily, yet she could not face returning to live on the meagre pension which most certainly would not provide a roof of her own over her head.

'Goodnight, Mrs Burton. We won't bother you for a late drink. I doubt if either of us will sleep much. I at least won't be going to bed for a long time.' The Colonel wanted her to go, as she was irritating him beyond endurance.

She closed the door behind her. Quint startled them by staring after her and growling loudly. He often gave vent to soft complaints when the housekeeper came near, but this was an unusually loud protest.

'She didn't even ask about Sapphire,' Roger said. Angrily he rummaged in the top drawer of his desk, producing a small pack of tobacco. He rammed it into his pipe as if he bore it a grudge.

'I'm smoking and I don't give a damn if she does leave. I can't call this house my own.'

A few minutes later he made a face, and knocked it out against the fire grate. Quint jumped, startled.

'Either I've lost the taste or this muck is stale; I've had it months.'

Lyan felt as if they were sitting at a wake, mourning the dead. The night hours dragged on so slowly. Time was indeed standing still. He glanced out of the window at the moonlit glade. Silver slipped into view like a ghost in the night, an exotic creature that brightened the darkness, light glancing on his white coat.

The schoolmaster longed for the quiet woods, but the Colonel needed company. He was sure that if he did not stay the man might console himself with too much whisky and then there would be trouble in the morning.

The Colonel switched on the television set and they watched a late-night film, neither of them taking in a single word. Both of them had their thoughts on Sapphire, wondering if she would ever come home again. She dominated their minds.

The endless night gave way to a bleak dawn. Heavy-eyed, the two men went to their own rooms to shower and shave and dress in fresh clothes, and met again at the breakfast-table, neither of them with any appetite. They rarely ate together in the mornings, Lyan, usually up first, contenting himself with coffee and toast which he made for himself. There were a percolator and a toaster on the dining-room sideboard.

Dorothy Burton brought in the food, her face grim. She sniffed, smelling the aftermath of whisky and tobacco. She put the plates down with an impatient bang, and then walked to the window and flung it wide. Quint, seeing a chance of freedom and an opportunity to search for Sapphire, ran towards it.

'Damn you, woman! I've no desire to lose my other dog

too,' the Colonel said, grabbing his collar and slamming the window shut. He glared at her.

She stared at him, startled. He had never raised his voice to her before. She walked out of the door, shutting it with a decisive sound that was not quite a bang. All that fuss over a dog, she thought bitterly as she returned to the kitchen and began to peel potatoes as if they were enemies she had to subdue.

Both men were waiting for the time to pass so that they could phone for news. Quint, given unusual privileges, was lying on the rug, his nose on his paws, his eyes distant. He followed the Colonel as if glued to his leg, in desperate need of company and reassurance.

Saturdays were usually busy for both men, the Colonel at work in the grounds, Lyan marking books. Both felt as if in limbo, waiting for news, yet dreading what they might be told.

Mac had said he would wait for them to call, so they stared in dismay when the phone rang during breakfast. It could only be bad news. The Colonel walked to answer it with considerable reluctance, glancing at Quint who seemed even more subdued. He had shown little interest in his morning walk, and again left his food untouched.

Lyan, watching closely, saw the man give a small sigh of relief. Not the vet.

'Jan has twisted his ankle. Put his foot down a rabbit-hole. He can only hobble,' the Colonel said. 'He'd promised to take Torran's paintings and his carvings to Melissa as she's off on a trip on Monday. Torran is going; he's worried. She has panic attacks when she goes into the village. He thought they'd vanish, but he says she's seemed worse recently. He hasn't told her about Sapphire yet.'

'I'll walk Quint, and buy a newspaper. Be natural enough to meet her,' Lyan said. Both German Shepherds were as well trained as any dogs could be. He picked up a leash. Quint stared at him, but showed no sign of excitement.

'I'll ring the vet before you go.' The Colonel dialled, and Lyan listened anxiously, hearing the ringing tone that seemed to continue endlessly. He sighed with relief when a voice answered.

'She's still alive. He wants to keep her in, and watch her. She's awake, but not very alert, not even a tail-wag when he spoke to her and she knows him well. We just have to wait and see.'

There was hopelessness in his voice.

'Come with me,' Lyan said. 'Or I'll leave Quint with you.'

'Take him. It'll distract him. I'll finish clearing the pool. Nothing like hard work . . .' He did not want to discuss Sapphire. He walked off, suddenly old, stooping a little, and Lyan was overwhelmed by utter fury, hating the poisoner and wishing him every ill in the world.

It was easy enough to watch the cottage through binoculars and see Torran start down the trail. She was dressed in jeans and a sleeveless hand-knitted pullover, a big felt satchel slung across her back. Lyan followed, taking time in catching her up. He did not want his presence to seem anything other than accidental.

A soft wind stirred the bushes, and Silver joined her, stepping delicately, often pausing to sniff the air. His restless ears listened to the sounds in the trees. Torran wished he could accompany her all the way. The woods were familiar, were home, but the village was an alien place where cold eyes stared at her and nobody spoke.

And someone hated her and wrote letters.

The ground was springy beneath her feet. It was a rare sunny day without a cloud in the sky. The stag paused, his quick eyes noting a movement. A squirrel ran across their path and up a nearby tree, and the deer relaxed. The wind was a soft song in the branches, keeping them company.

91

She did not want to reach the village. Jan's sprain was not bad and he would soon be about again, but they needed the money that Melissa would bring them. Her grandfather refused to make any demands on the social services, other than taking his pension. Anything else he regarded as charity. They would earn and pay their way.

She knew nothing of the trust in her name which Jan was keeping intact for when he was no longer able to provide for her.

The path wound through the trees. Silver stood still, his ears working overtime, forwards, backwards, listening, and then with a quick bound he was out of sight, leaving Torran marooned on the path, her heart beating fast.

Then she too caught the sound of chanting.

'Here comes the wicked witch, the wicked witch, the wicked old witch. Here comes the wicked witch. It's high time the wicked old witch was dead.'

She froze against the tree trunk behind her, afraid to move, afraid of the singing that mocked her, not knowing where they were.

'Here comes the wicked witch . . .' The high trebles told their own story. Lyan, not far behind Torran, knew the culprits at once, recognising both voices: his terrible pair of horrors. He saw the bushes quiver and with a few swift strides was down the path, the dog beside him. Quint had at first plodded quietly at heel, showing no sign of interest in the smells on the path. Lyan had begun to wish he had not brought him. His apathy was unnerving.

The chanting and Lyan's quick action triggered the German Shepherd, who nosed into the bushes and barked. The two children exploded out in terror.

'Guard,' he said, as he seized them by the shoulders and turned them to face him. As he thought: both could be depended on for any mischief in the village or at school. Their recent friendship worried him. He sighed. Lucy Cartwright, the farmer's ten-year-old daughter, and

Davey Prentice, six months older, whose father was their local councillor.

'Stop that at once,' he said, aware of Torran, white-faced, watching them, unable to move. She was still leaning against a tree, feeling sick, panic returning, so that her legs were quivering and her breath came too fast and she thought she might faint. The feeling of helplessness infuriated her, but she had not discovered how to control it.

'Not doing anything wrong,' Davey said.

'Sticks and stones may break your bones but names will never hurt you.' Lucy grinned up at him, her small plump face smug with the knowledge that anything he did to her would cause him trouble and gain her only sympathy. She was a child, wasn't she? And he was a large adult, maybe offering violence. Her mum would have something to say about that.

'Don't they hurt?' Lyan asked, useless anger making him long to shake both of them. He wished they lived forty years ago when a recalcitrant child could be reprimanded with a slapped bottom and nobody would even criticise. He released them and Quint growled, sensing the atmosphere.

'If that dog touches us, my dad will report you and him and he'll be taken away and put in kennels and then put to sleep and you'll never seen him again,' Davey said.

'Or my dad will shoot him,' said Lucy. 'He's been worrying the cattle.'

Lyan, who knew that neither dog was ever out alone and that that accusation was a total lie, was shaken with fury. Children needed discipline, and that was something neither of these had ever known, though he suspected Lucy was afraid of her father.

'Suppose I told you that you're the ugliest girl I've ever seen and will never be able to hold down a good job or even make someone a good wife? Doesn't that hurt?'

'It's not true.' Lucy stared at him, her eyes angry. 'She *is* a witch anyway. Nobody else walks round with a ghost deer.'

'What I said about you isn't true, any more than what you're saying is true. I'll see you both in school in break on Monday.' He almost said that Silver was no ghost, but maybe the story protected the animal from harm. No one would shoot a phantom.

'I'll tell my mum what you said about me. She'll sort you out.'

Lyan, who knew the father, but the mother only slightly, doubted if she would sort anybody out and was pretty certain Lucy would not dare tell Jim about the encounter. All the same, he knew he had been unwise. Lucy was an unpredictable child at the best of times and given to lying competently and plausibly when the mood seized her.

'Go home, and leave Miss Ardan alone,' he said.

Quint, worried by the atmosphere, growled menacingly. Lyan quieted him, and watched as the two walked off down the ride, Davey turning to put out his tongue when at a safe distance.

'Thank you,' Torran said, rallying herself. 'I ought not to mind, but I do.' She was still trembling, her face white. She swallowed, trying to make an effort to recover.

'I'm not surprised. You are going to the village, aren't you? I'll walk with you. I need a newspaper. I don't think any child would dare torment you with the two of us beside you.'

They walked together down the path. A blackbird sang suddenly, startling the dog, and he barked.

The children were angry. Lyan had spoiled their fun. Both gained considerable pleasure from tormenting, having discovered early that that gave them power. Lucy, who found people baffling, never teased the animals. It was the thought of Torran harming them that triggered her anger.

The schoolmaster was vulnerable. Well away from both Torran and Lyan, hidden among the trees, Lucy's clear voice rang out.

'Scarface. Yah. Scarface.'

Davey joined in, the voices echoing from the hilltop.

'Scarface. Scarface. Scarface.'

Torran stared at him, appalled. She had not looked closely at him before, had only seen him at night, and he had been careful to keep the damaged side of his face away from her. Now she saw the puckered skin, the tightness of his lips, the pain in his eyes and the hand that went to cover his cheek.

Quint barked, a deep reverberating roar, and the children, suddenly afraid the schoolmaster might release the dog, raced down the hill to the sanctuary of Jim Cartwright's big barn where they hid in the straw, giggling.

Torran felt as if she had come suddenly out of a deep mist, where events only affected her and other people had no existence. Lyan's pain was her pain. She knew he had been shot and had retired from the police, but had never thought about the trauma that must have surrounded both events.

She didn't know what to do. Quick to sense pain in an animal, she felt as if she were now confronted, not with a man, but with a wounded beast, and forgot all fear of him. She came forward and, very gently, put her hand to the scarred cheek and stroked it, a feather-light touch, offering comfort.

Lyan, who had never before shared his misery, took the hand and held it briefly, unable to thank her and hoping she understood that he sensed her own need to help him.

Quint, impatient, pulled on the lead and Lyan smiled, glad of the opportunity to gloss over what had happened. They began to walk, aware of birdsong and a squirrel that stopped to look at them and then, seeing the dog, fled up a tree.

They both laughed.

'Quint's learnt that squirrels are faster than he is. The squirrel has probably learnt it isn't wise to come down to the ground with a dog about,' Lyan said.

'Where's Sapphire? I've never seen one dog by itself before. He's not nearly so lively without her. Is she with the Colonel?'

'Someone poisoned her. She's at the vet's. We don't know yet if she'll survive.'

Torran stared at him. Poison! Threatening the foxes and the badgers, the cats that wandered in the woods as well as those that had long ago gone wild; even birds that might peck at the bait. Suppose the fox cubs were still alive and found it when foraging? Or the badger cubs? She had thought that little worse could happen, but it seemed there was no end to the horrors that lay in store for them all.

'Where did she get it from? Have any other animals suffered?'

'One of the Cartwright cats. That died. Mac thinks someone may have laid bait for rats. Or the cat could have eaten a poisoned mouse. Not Sapphire, though.'

Torran looked up at him with agonised eyes.

'The little grey cat used to come to us and take the food I left for the birds. Jim Cartwright never feeds his cats. Jan says he says they have to earn their keep and live on mice and rats. Suppose she took it from my bird table? When Quint and Sapphire are free they rob that too, if the Colonel doesn't remember.'

Jan had made the bird table for her. It was built in three parts, starting with a small platform on which food was put out for the larger birds, while the uppermost section was much smaller and netted to keep away squirrels. It was always stocked with bread, bacon rind, meat dripping and scraps left from their meals. It would be easy enough to add to it, and no one would notice an extra crust or lump of meat.

They walked in silence, contemplating disaster. Were Quint and Sapphire the intended victims? Had someone been watching, intending to burgle the Colonel's home when both dogs were dead?

Lyan, who had been afraid that there might be bait scattered on the path, had kept Quint leashed. He handed the lead to Torran.

'He's good company,' he said, hoping that the need to think about the dog might soothe whatever fears were dominating his companion. He missed Sapphire, who always led, merry-eyed, nosing in the undergrowth, first to find a new scent, her body vibrant with eager life.

He didn't want to think about her. He needed to change the subject, but found himself at a loss, nervously aware of Torran's unease.

'I never walk in the woods without thinking of a poem by Robert Frost,' he said, after another far too long and silent interval. "The woods are lovely, dark and deep . . ."'

She smiled suddenly, a vivid lightening of her face that darkened her eyes, a glow brightening them. The deep brown was almost black, reminding him of the evening sky before the stars came out.

She capped his quotation.

' "But I have promises to keep, / And miles to go before I sleep". I love that too.' He was too shaken to respond. Another poem drifted into his head, but he did not say it aloud:

> I did but see her passing by
> And yet I love her till I die.

He was too old for such foolishness, but the words stayed in the back of his mind and he was painfully aware of

97

every movement she made. He had captured her night after night, on his film, playing with fox cubs, watching badger cubs, teasing the dog fox with a glove that he snatched and carried away, his head high, his eyes gleeful. She was his secret passion and only now did he realise it.

There were shrubs in blossom in the village gardens, clematis flowering against a wall, and a wild riot of colour in the flowerbeds outside the vicarage windows.

'I'm all right now,' Torran said. The colour had come back to her face, but Lyan noticed that she kept her head down as they walked through the village, avoiding curious eyes. He sighed. The witch woman and the schoolmaster. Tongues would chatter.

'Come and have coffee with us.' Melissa appeared suddenly from behind her garden wall. She had watched in disbelief as the two walked down the street. Torran had never come to see her before and she was astounded that she was not alone. She was always uneasy when Melissa visited, reminding her of a bird poised to fly away at any sudden movement.

Lyan hesitated.

'We'd like company, wouldn't we, Torran?' Melissa asked. 'It's good to see you, but is Jan all right?'

Torran smiled at them, unexpectedly appreciating Melissa's concern and the thought of a longer time with the schoolmaster.

'He's sprained his ankle. Otherwise he's fine. Do stay, Lyan. Have you time?'

He was anxious to get back, worried about the Colonel and afraid that Sapphire might have died. Neither thought could be expressed.

He could not, in all decency, refuse.

Nine

Quint led the way to the little sitting-room, familiar with the vicarage from visits with the Colonel. Tia, the Siamese, yowled a greeting and walked over to nose the dog, happy to see him again.

Lyan had never been in the vicarage before and was enchanted by Melissa's bright colours and the brilliant drapes flung over chairs and settee and hung at the windows.

There were no pictures, but the walls were covered in small round framed plaques, each of them depicting tiny animals made of grass-heads and fircones, surrounded by small pressed flowers and furry catkins, each one a vivid woodland scene.

'My mother used to make them. I've been trying to collect them from her old clients,' Melissa said, as Lyan walked over to study one of two hedgehogs and a mouse. 'I love them. They were part of my childhood.'

On a shelf that went right round the room, a foot below the ceiling, were glass animals: a delicate swan, a prowling cat, an otter standing on its hind legs, a seal, and a lion. There seemed to be hundreds of them, some of blown glass, some that appeared to be carved out of a giant crystal, only part of the animal in relief. A cluster of green frogs, varying in size from half an inch to six inches, caught the light from the window.

Torran settled herself on a seat in the big bay, as far away from the other inhabitants of the room as possible. Melissa took the satchel and opened it, exclaiming at the wooden animals: a fox, a prancing horse, a seal, a goat, and a squirrel sitting on its hind legs, eating a nut.

'They're always so alive,' she said, holding up another horse that stood on three legs, scratching himself with the fourth. Jan put in glass eyes that glittered, catching the light, adding to the seeming reality.

Lyan had wondered about the paintings until he saw them. A fox watched as her cubs played under a full moon, the light glinting on fern fronds that masked an enchanting small face. Moonlight danced on water that rippled beyond tree trunks mottled with light.

In a second picture the vixen stood on the trunk of a fallen tree, looking into the distance, and two cubs, half-hidden beneath it, stared, one of them snarling. The vixen was alert, poised to leap, poised to take her offspring to safety. The half-grown bodies were tense, ears pricked, wary.

In the last the fox stood alone, among trees just showing the first buds of spring, while the ground around him was starred with primroses. He recognised Blacktip, standing there in the prime of his life, and felt a pang seize him at the thought of such beauty ruined.

'They'll all sell well,' Melissa said, handing them cups of coffee and buttered scones. 'They're marvellous. I can sell as many as you can paint.'

'These are good,' Lyan said with appreciation, referring to the food, as he felt that comments on Torran's pictures might not be welcome. The delicate bone china worried him. It was so fragile, almost translucent, that he was afraid it would break as he handled it. Torran was tracing the pattern of forget-me-nots and honeysuckle with one finger, entranced.

'WI. I'm no cook.' Melissa was wearing fawn trousers and a vivid blue blouse, a coral necklace round her neck. The tawny hair was tied in a pony tail, instead of being neatly coiled in a chignon, as it often was in deference to the villagers.

'I try to be seemly,' she occasionally said to her husband when he commented on her clothes. 'I can't go about in long tweed skirts and twin sets. I do need to be partly me. I don't wear trousers in church.' She wore bright suits, which horrified the more soberly clad village women who seemed to think that God preferred dark colours. She suspected that everything she did would meet with censure, so it was no use bothering.

'I'm damned if I do, and damned if I don't,' she said. Donald never interfered. Life without her was unthinkable and he was afraid that if he criticised she would go, feeling that she was an exotic bird that had come to perch in his home, and could so easily fly away from him. Melissa would have been astounded if he had shared that thought.

She picked up a tiny mug from the table, half gleaming with silvery brightness, half of it still dull and tarnished. The cleaning cloth and polish lay beside it, together with a small brush.

'What do you think of this?' she asked Lyan.

'A christening mug? It's a pretty thing. Do people still give such things as presents?'

'Some do. Most are more practical now. I got it from the disposal of an old woman's bits and pieces. Her son wanted to get rid of everything fast and held the sale himself in the house, people coming and taking what they wanted. It was ridiculous: she had some valuable stuff there which he let go for a song. This had been in the family for centuries, handed down from generation to generation.'

She sighed.

'I hate that sort of sale. It always makes me wonder what will happen to all the things I collect and love when I'm dead. Who will treasure them as I do? Will they be sold off for almost nothing or, worse, just thrown away?'

Quint came to sit by Torran's side, looking up at her, his brown eyes pleading. She bent and hugged him. Tai, as if aware of the dog's unhappiness, cuddled against him, purring noisily.

'He does miss Sapphire.' Torran wished she could comfort him.

'Why didn't you bring her?' Melissa asked and listened with horror when Lyan told her.

'They're the Colonel's children; he'll be distraught if anything happens to her. Poor old boy, he adores his dogs.'

Lyan glanced at Torran, whose eyes were cast down. He couldn't bear to think of Sapphire, maybe already dead. He picked up the little mug, admiring the elegant shape, the delicate tracery and the intricate handle.

'It's beautiful. I don't think I could bear to part with it. Will you sell it?' he asked, knowing how much the Colonel admired her expertise. She had found a wonderful silver tankard which she had given him for Christmas the year before.

'It'll help pay for a new altar cloth. We need one badly. Only don't tell the village: they wouldn't approve of a vicar's wife in trade.'

'I must go back,' Torran said, suddenly overwhelmed and feeling trapped, panic starting again. 'My grandfather needs me. He can't walk far at all, and there's so much to do.'

'Shall I come with you?' Lyan was anxious, but didn't want to force himself on her.

'I'll be all right alone.' She had to make herself face the world sometime. She couldn't hide away for ever, but she was aware of a fast-beating heart and a desire to run back to the security of the cottage and Jan's comforting presence. She hated this strange disability that seemed to have altered her personality and limited her life, but no matter how hard she tried, the fear always returned.

They watched as she walked down the little drive. Lyan was bothered about her, wondering if he ought to follow.

'I suspect agoraphobia.' Melissa picked up the mug and the little brush and began to rub hard, making Lyan wonder fleetingly and absurdly if perhaps she might produce a genie. 'Jan says she won't see a doctor. Says there's nothing wrong and she doesn't want to go through her life half-doped with pills that probably do more harm than good. She hates any form of medicine except for natural ones.'

She sighed, overcome at a world so full of problems that neither she nor her husband could ever hope to solve.

'Jan worries, especially about what would become of her if anything happened to him. I even arranged for the doctor to have his car break down near the cottage and ask to use the phone to ring for help. She was out of the back door before he came in at the front.'

Torran, out in the fresh air and on her way home to the woods, felt an immense pressure lift from her. She had felt stifled in the little sitting-room. She wondered suddenly if the cubs might still be alive and in a den that was perilously close to the Cartwright farm.

She followed the track through the woods, along the edge of the farthermost field, intending to inspect the den and see if it were occupied. There would be traces outside of their kills. Maybe Jim Cartwright had found it already and killed the cubs.

A hare sprang out of the tussock near her feet and bounded away. She paused to watch a kestrel hanging on the wind, and wonder how he could hover for so long.

A sudden agonised squealing from beyond the hedge startled her. It was repeated and, stimulated by the knowledge of an animal in pain, she ran down the path towards the five-barred gate.

The little Springer Spaniel was crouched in the grass, her eyes terrified as Jim Cartwright thrashed her savagely with a riding-whip. Torran forgot fear. She vaulted the gate and raced across the field, scooping up the dog in her arms and seizing the whip.

He stared at her, astounded that anyone dared to defy him. She was transformed into a fury he did not recognise. Her eyes blazed at him, the pale cheeks flushed and angry.

'Leave her alone. I'll report you. I'll buy the bitch from you. She's obviously no good to you. She won't do as you want after treating her like that. She'll be too terrified.'

He rallied, enraged in his turn by being challenged, and by a woman at that. His women knew their place, he made very sure of that, and if they dared to defy him they suffered. He was a big man. His belly hung over his dirty trouser-tops. His enormous feet were encased in giant muddy wellingtons. His red face was flushed. A rising wind tormented his tangled, greasy hair. He glared at Torran, transferring his anger from the dog.

'She's stupid. Useless.' He suddenly realised what she had said. She had offered money. Cupidity won.

'How much will you give for her?'

'A hundred pounds.' Torran knew she was being reckless but was sure he wouldn't part with the spaniel for less. She dared not leave her with him as she knew he would subject the little animal to his fury as soon as she was gone. 'You can call for it tomorrow evening. I don't have it on me. I'm taking the dog now.'

The bitch had come to him as a pup in payment for hay and sacks of potatoes. A hundred pounds was an unexpected bonus and far more than she was worth to him.

'Take her, and see the money's ready, or I'll report her stolen.'

Torran intended to insist on a receipt in writing. She didn't trust the man. The purchase would absorb most of her savings, but she spent little and Melissa would have more for her when she sold the next batch of paintings.

'What's her name?'

'Not got one. Call her "Dog" when I want her, or whistle. She doesn't need a name.'

Torran lifted the trembling spaniel. She was so angry that she dared not say anything more and her fury helped her to forget her own fears. The bitch had no muscle or flesh under her coat, and weighed so little that she suspected she was half-starved. She was afraid that if she put her down she might run off.

Jim Cartwright watched her walk away, amazed at himself. He scratched his head with black-rimmed nails.

'Well, I'll be double damned,' he said, astounded at meeting a woman who stood up to him.

Torran was trembling as she walked up the hill. Jan would be as angry as she, she knew, never having any doubt about his reception of the waif. She thought of him with sudden affection, her rock on which she could rely, always. The confrontation had brought memory of the night they stood together, hidden in the trees, not daring to move lest they be seen, while the emissaries from hell tortured her family and their farm-hands, and their women and children.

She had been away longer than he expected. Jan, never easy when she was out on her own, watched anxiously through the window, and breathed a deep sigh of relief as he saw her walking up the path, the spaniel in her arms.

'I bought her from Jim Cartwright,' she said, coming into the room. 'He was beating her and she's more than half-starved.'

She put the bitch down on the hearthrug. She immediately fled, retreating under the lowest chair, completely out of sight.

Jan eased his leg, and set his teeth as pain knifed through his ankle.

'You've bought another headache,' he commented, knowing very well that his granddaughter could never resist any animal in distress. The shed at the back was full of invalids in cages. Luckily most of them were temporary guests and released as soon as fit. The latest was a baby owl fallen from the nest. It was proving difficult to feed as Torran hated having to provide it with mice or day-old chicks.

She piled logs on the fire, as the room was cold. The thick walls of the cottage seemed to take weeks to absorb the summer heat. She prepared a plate of beef and horseradish sandwiches, and set down food for the dog on the far end of the rug, hoping that the little bitch would come out and eat, but there was neither sight nor sound from her.

That evening Torran helped Jan to his room, and wrapped his ankle in a poultice soaked with arnica lotion. He had opted for a very early bedtime, finding it less painful to lie still.

'Watch the ground when you go out for logs, or to your hospital,' he said. 'I put my foot into a rabbit hole. They're making burrows near the vegetable garden.'

Her chores completed, Torran settled in the quiet room, determined to stay there all night if necessary. She began to sketch, drawing small animal faces—rabbits and hares and foxes and stoats, weasels and deer, and a spaniel puppy, long-eared, eyes glinting with mischief.

The little spaniel had started to creep out from under the chair, impelled by the food, when there was a bang on the door, and she retreated fast. Torran opened it, keeping on the chain, and stared at Jim Cartwright, who, half-drunk, had decided to come for his money.

'I told you tomorrow.'

'I want it now, or I take the bitch back.'

She had only twenty pounds in her purse. Jan had fifty in his wallet. They were thirty pounds short. She went to the little jewel-case and took out the ring she had been wearing when the raiders struck. She never wore it now.

It was worth far more than she had offered. She felt a slight pang: her stepfather had given it to her. But the little life was worth more than a pretty band of gold and a few jewels.

'You can sell that to make up the difference,' she said. 'I want a receipt.'

She had no intention of opening the door wide to let him in. Hastily she wrote out a note and gave it to him, with the pen, so that he could sign.

He read it:

'I acknowledge the receipt of £70 and a diamond and sapphire ring in return for one Springer Spaniel bitch.' She had added the date.

Jim looked at the money and examined the ring, his small eyes sparkling. The girl was a fool. It was worth far more than thirty pounds. He scrawled his name and handed her back the paper.

'Print it too,' she said. The signature was almost unreadable. He did as she asked, smirking at the thought of the money he would obtain for the ring.

Torran did not relax until his footsteps died away. Given the choice between a piece of jewellery and a pup, she would always choose the pup. The exchange was all in her favour: she had been longing for a dog.

She warmed some soup, adding two tablespoons to the bowl of dogfood, hoping the heat would intensify the smell and bring the bitch out again. She had probably lived in a kennel, certainly not in the house, and there would be training problems as she was unlikely to be clean.

Outside the window Silver, anxious for company, drummed his hoof against the door. Moonlight shone on his white coat and gleamed in his dark eyes. Torran took carrots from the bin and fed him, knowing he delighted in the taste. When he had finished she stamped her foot on the ground, a signal she had taught him from babyhood that meant 'Strangers about. Hide.'

She did not want him to think that all people would treat him as she had. After feeding the pheasants she always clapped her hands so that they flew off. Fear was vital for survival and she had no intention of making any animal trust all humans.

She came back into the room. The spaniel was crouched over the bowl, feeding. She stared up at her rescuer, her eyes agonised, as if expecting a kick or a blow. Torran sat on the rug, the fire hot on her face, and made no movement. The bitch needed a name. She could not imagine anyone living with a dog, even for a few days, without giving it an identity.

The little dog was brown and white, small for her breed, her long ears, in need of a wash, coated with matted food. She probably had fleas, but any spray would terrify her. Her coat was rough and dull, and her ribs protruded.

She finished her food. Torran did not move. She had a piece of cheese in her hand, which was lying on her knee. The room was lit only by firelight which glinted on the plates on the dresser, on the polished arms of the battered settee, on the stool which she had painted with flowers and ferns, and on Jan's worktable, on which was the half-carved figure of a charging bull, head down, its body full of life.

The bitch was still crouched over the empty plate. When Torran looked at her she slid her eyes away, and turned her head, wishing to be invisible. There had been a spaniel on the farm when she was a tiny girl. What was her name? Torran had a vision of her stepfather walking with the little dog beside him, she looking up at him and he laughing down at her.

Amber. There were only happy memories associated with her. The dog crept to her, and took the cheese from her hand, so gently that it was almost a breath, the lips scarcely opening. Torran began to stroke the small body, talking softly.

'Amber. You'll have to learn that name, learn all kinds of things you don't know now; but we'll teach you, little girl.'

She was very careful not to look into the brown eyes, knowing that, to this dog, even a loving stare would be interpreted as a threat and a challenge. She hated the feel of the ribby little body beneath her hands, but it was no use feeding her up too soon as that would make her ill.

She needed to meet all kinds of people, or she would never grow out of her fears. It would take time, Torran knew.

A small tentative tongue licked the hand which smelled of cheese. Torran added more logs to the fire, took a cushion from the chair, and stretched herself on the rug. The dog crept into her arms.

She fell asleep, the small, warm body cuddled against her. She woke once and built the fire again. The night was cold and summer was slow to come. Lying there, drowsy, she had a vision of herself and the dog, building confidence together.

The spaniel in her arms was an immense comfort. For the first time for months Torran felt a small ray of hope. Maybe, as she taught this dog, she too would learn to forget fear.

Ten

It was two days before the vet would allow Sapphire home. She was far from fit, and shaky on her legs, so that the Colonel carried her and put her on the rug. Quint, over-joyed to see her, wanted to romp and found it difficult to understand that his playmate had no desire whatever to join in any games. At last, tired of coaxing her, he lay down, watching her, his eyes never leaving her, aware of every movement she made.

She came out into the garden on her lead, as did Quint now. Neither was allowed to run off and explore. Nobody knew the source of the poison or where there might be more. She was offered fish and rice, moistened with milk, which at first she refused, taking little interest in anything that went on around her.

Quint, sure her food was better than his, tried to take it from her, so that in the end Lyan gave him his meals outside while the Colonel coaxed Sapphire to eat. He had little success at first. Torran, for the first time, came to visit, bringing with her a phial of Rescue Remedy.

The Colonel, not at all sure of this strange offering, felt that it could do no harm and added it to the syringe of glucose and water with which he dosed the bitch every hour. Five days after she came home there was little change, and Mac could offer no reassurance.

She was still sore, her inside raw, and she had little desire to eat and risk pain until, on the sixth day, des-perate because she seemed to be sinking into apathy, Roger opened a tin of red salmon and added the juice. She had always adored it and, as a treat, the two dogs had bread soaked in the liquid. Tinned salmon was a stand-by meal when Mrs Burton was off duty.

Sapphire sniffed the food warily, always cautious of anything new. Suddenly her eyes brightened, as she recognised her favourite taste. For the first time she ate with a will and licked the plate clean. Next time some of the salmon was added to the fish and within two weeks she began to look more like her normal sleek self.

Jan brought some of the herbal mixture that Torran made up for her own injured animals. That, to both men's surprise, the dog lapped eagerly and asked for more.

Neither of the German Shepherds could understand why they were no longer allowed to run free through the woods, or why the leashes were always on, even in the garden.

'I feel I'm being neurotic,' the Colonel said. 'But next time we might not be so lucky . . . if there is a next time. Who knows what she found, or why it was there?'

Their unease was increased when Jan received another anonymous letter. There was no stamp. The malice had to be local.

Only Torran knew of the missives that were pinned to the door on the nights she was out. She began to feel that she was being watched by someone who knew every movement, but still said nothing. She was unaware that Jan in turn was keeping from her those he intercepted.

Lyan wondered if Lucy Cartwright were capable of thinking up such a scheme. She and Davey now behaved fairly well in class, but exchanged knowing looks and grinned smugly when they spoke to him, careful always to add 'sir' in such a way that it was insolent.

At times he felt that they were changelings, little fiends, and not human at all. They put snails and slugs in Shelley's desk, knowing she was terrified of them, and Davey brought a spider and hid it in Mark's lunchbox. Mark, who was phobic about the creatures, was so disturbed that

Lyan instituted a daily search in case there was another.

One night he glimpsed the little family on the hill. The cat was still with them and he was sure now that this was Elf's orphaned litter. The cat had profited by her disasters and become wily, guarding her new family with deep devotion. She saw Lyan and moved them yet higher, into dense cover, utilising a long-discarded den under rocks that, cave-like, needed no further excavation.

Ric still needed an extra share of her concern. He was always ready to explore beyond his capabilities, intent on savouring every smell, every new sight. She had to hunt for much more of her time to keep the growing cubs fed. She brought mouse and rat and dormouse, pheasant chicks and small birds, fledged but not yet skilful enough at flying.

She was very weary. Her fur was shabby, her underparts almost bare, and, since she had had no release from milk when she lost her first litters, she had also lost her shape.

The cubs had not yet ventured far down the slopes and remained unseen except by Lyan. He did not want anyone to know of their presence. He did not see Torran, who was busy trying to help Amber overcome her fears. She stayed near the cottage, partly in the hope of seeing the unknown message-writer, partly in the hope that her presence would act as a deterrent, a hope that seemed to be realised as she found no more of the fear-inducing envelopes.

*   *   *

The days went by and the cubs thrived and grew. Their constant romping strengthened small muscles. Even Ric began to learn caution, mostly through very narrow escapes due entirely to his vigilant foster-mother and her devastating claws. He still had to be herded back because he journeyed too far in his explorations.

Disaster threatened one day when the weasel made a bid for a rather larger meal than usual. The little animal began to weave, to somersault and twist into the air, clowning. The cubs watched, fascinated, gradually drawing nearer to this enticing creature. He spun in a mazy dance, faster and faster, until he was a flicker of movement and not an animal at all. Birds collected. The little cat, returning with a rat in her mouth, dropped her prey, knowing that here was immense danger.

Her leap took the weasel in mid-air, knocking him to the ground. For a few minutes they fought, the cat raking and scratching, hissing her anger, the weasel twisting and trying to bite. Mother instinct gave her strength, so that she drove him off. The birds had long gone. The cubs sat in the clearing, appalled by the din. When their foster-mother, her wounds bleeding, hissed at them, they went meekly to their den and curled up, chastened, while she licked at her injuries, and finally slept, exhausted by the battle.

The weasel found the rat and ate it. He left the little family alone, aware that he could not compete with the cat. Within twenty-four hours, though plagued by a limp due to a bad bite on her leg, she was hunting again, bringing back live prey for the cubs to learn to kill for themselves.

Below the den, on the hill, the hinds were edgy, many of their young new-born and very vulnerable. The cat was aware of the birth scents and of the babies lying deep in the undergrowth, but knew they were too large for her to tackle.

There were others on the hill. The two men with the terriers had talked in the pub at Pyneton about the deer in the woods. At the beginning of July poachers came with guns. Lyan was not out that night, and Torran was busy with Amber, so that nobody saw them. They all heard the shots and worried, but knew better than to investigate.

113

Silver, out in the early morning, smelled blood, kicked up his heels and was about to run when he heard a forlorn, frantic bleating. Investigating the bracken, he found a tiny fawn. The bloodstains on the ground had come from her mother, whose body was now on its way to Pyneton.

The baby was only two days old. He looked down at her and nosed her, bringing comfort. She stood, a little unsteadily, and, as he walked down the hill, kept close beside him, desperate for contact. Twice she tried to find a source of milk and was baffled by his refusal to let her frantic mouth hunt between his legs.

Torran, looking out of the window, was relieved to see him walk across the clearing and into the garden. She had been afraid that he was the victim of last night's raid. She did not notice the fawn, hidden behind him, its small legs very tired.

He rapped on the door with his hoof, the imperious knock that always brought her, and then stood back. She stared in dismay at the tiny animal, guessing that she had been orphaned in the night.

Silver led the way to his own old shelter, where the baby dropped onto the straw. Large eyes looked up at Torran, and the forlorn bleat edged her into anger. She had not noticed Amber, who had followed her, and was staring at the newcomer. The little bitch walked over to the fawn, nosed her, then washed the small head and curled up beside her.

Silver, his duty done, returned to his own favourite bush and settled beneath it, keeping an eye on the cottage and the spaniel and fawn. He had no fear of Torran's other protégés. Amber now accepted Jan as well, but ran and hid if anyone else came near. She still hated eye contact and not even Torran could look at her. If she did, the spaniel still turned her back and sat, gazing into the distance, pretending nobody was there. She hid from all the other animals, and Silver alarmed her, especially when he rapped for attention.

Torran heated milk and filled a bottle. The little one at first found the process difficult to understand and refused to drink until the teat was squeezed, directing a stream of milk into her mouth. Some of it spilled. Amber licked the small muzzle clean, and then watched as at last the baby realised what she should do and sucked vigorously, emptying it fast and bleating for more.

In the next few days the two became inseparable, Amber insisting on sharing the outside shed and the straw at night. She brought her small charge faithfully to the back door of the cottage when it was feeding time, apparently knowing by instinct when the fawn was hungry and the bottle would be ready.

Silver, intrigued, came to visit, and though the little bitch was alarmed she would not leave her self-imposed duty. She growled softly, lest he harm her companion. The baby deer nosed him, lifting her small head, trying to reach him, and he bent to her and his touch comforted her.

Within days she was skittish with youth and raced round the clearing, bounding up to the big deer. Amber was suddenly imbued with a desire to join the fun and Torran spent hours watching the three play together, chasing and giving chase, ending always in the newcomer returning, exhausted, to her bed in the straw with Amber on guard beside her.

Silver had taught her to tap on the door, and now, when she considered it time for her bottle, she stepped daintily across the yard and rapped imperiously, demanding an immediate response, adding her hungry impatient bleat if Torran did not come at once. She pestered for her bottle, hammering on the fence with a hoof if it were not brought to her.

Within a few days she had earned the name of Miss

Impatience. Everyone called her Missie. Torran taught her to copy Silver and hide at once if she stamped her foot on the ground. Amber learned the signal and vanished with them. This worried her owner, in case there was poison around the cottage, but the little bitch always came fast now when called, and trotted into the garden with her charge.

The care of the animals was helping Torran forget her fears. Daytime was no longer so daunting and several times she walked with Lyan and Amber to visit Melissa, taking over the delivery of the little carvings and the paintings. Jan had recovered, but he thought that if he pretended the walk was too much for him Torran would go instead and overcome her phobia.

Lyan bought a painting from her, a picture of the springtime woods, the grey-barked trees warped and twisted, their lines softened by lichen. Beneath them the ground was covered with windflowers and primroses. New leaves glistened, wet with dew. The trees looming through the misty light rising from the ground were spectral, their mystery enhanced by the glimmer of the white stag, almost invisible, a ghost creature. In front of him, standing with his eyes curious and his body arrogant, was Blacktip at the height of his prime.

Within its frame was everything he treasured. He only had to look at it to feel soothed. The woods were there and when school ended he would walk in them, and rest his soul.

Summer had forgotten them. Grey days brought frequent rain. A gale broke branches off some of the trees, ending in lightning and thunder that terrified even Ric who crouched with the other cubs while the cat curled round them, soothing them because she had known such weather before and knew that it would end.

Silver curled up that night in the straw with Amber and Missie, his presence reassuring them. Amber crept against him, shivering, and hid her eyes when lightning flared across the sky. The thunder noise was the crashing reverberation of a thousand guns, deafening her.

The drumming rain kept intruders away. The trees fought the gale, their branches bending and groaning, alarming all the animals. Even the birds cried out in fear.

In the big house the Colonel and Lyan gave up all idea of sleep and sat together in companionable silence, sipping whisky and soda. Sapphire came for comfort to her master, overcoming her fear so long as she was with the men she loved. Quint, who was never bothered by natural noises, though he hated shouting, lay on the rug, happy to have company at an hour when humans normally slept.

Lightning flashed and flared across the sky and far off, in the woods, a fireball hit a tree and rent it in two with a crack that sent every beast still out scurrying for shelter, and kept the woods free from any life at all for several hours.

Torran woke and checked on the deer and the little spaniel. They looked at her with anxious eyes but seemed to show little fear of the din of the night. She offered Amber the chance to come indoors but she preferred to take care of her baby. The fact that Missie was several times bigger than her foster-mother did not seem to bother the spaniel at all. By the time Torran returned, Jan had made them both a hot drink and was standing at the window watching the sky.

'No wonder the ancients thought there were demons,' he said. 'On a night like this I can believe in anything: creatures from hell risen to make life impossible for us feeble humans.'

'My nurse used to tell me a story ... that there was nothing really to be afraid of because the angels were having a firework night and, being angels, the bangs and flashes had to be enormous, much bigger than anything on earth.'

'I'd forgotten you had a nurse. She sounds a sensible woman, you must have been very small.'

'I was about three. You hadn't come out to us then. Mum wasn't very well; Nerine was a baby, and she found it hard to look after me as well. I was too adventurous, always in scrapes and in terrible trouble because I brought all kinds of small animals into the house. I called the nurse Goo Goo, heaven knows why. She was really a sort of glorified *au pair*, doing a year's work before she went to college.'

'Alys Gould,' Jan said, suddenly enlightened. 'I'd forgotten all about her. Your mother told me of her. You were supposed to call her Miss Gould, as she didn't want to be known as Nanny, and nobody thought it appropriate for you to call her Alys. You couldn't get your tongue round it. They all called her Goo Goo in the end. She stayed the year, and used to send birthday and Christmas cards for a long time afterwards.'

'I thought she was wonderful. She had so much time to spare for me, and read me stories and helped me make all kinds of things from coloured paper. Mine were awful. She made wonderful little horses and owls. I cried for days when she went. Nobody else ever seemed to have much time for me till you came.'

'They were busy with the farm. It was far too much work for one couple, even with the amount of help they had. I worked flat out when I came out too. There was always something. A thousand head of cattle and your father insisted on being there when each one calved. Your mother did the paperwork.'

It was the first time they had talked of the past. Soon afterwards the storm died away, and the wind dropped. Torran went out into a rain-washed wood. Silver and Missie walked into the clearing and the fawn, seeing her, trotted over, demanding food. Torran laughed and knelt to hug Amber, who rewarded her with a lick on her face.

Lyan, passing on his way to school, saw them and treasured the memory during a day that was to prove more troublesome than any he had yet known.

Eleven

Lyan dreaded windy days. That year there seemed to be a season of gales at the end of the spring, so that the dogs were crazy with excitement, racing one another round the garden and pausing now and then to roll on the wet grass. The children were as bad: restless, uneasy, and very difficult to control. This particular day was one he was not likely to forget.

During the weeks since Sapphire had been poisoned they had evolved a routine, almost without discussion. Both men were early risers, unless Lyan had been night filming. The dogs were outside by six, the ground strewn with pieces of bread and meat.

For ten minutes each dog was led around, leashed, and sharply checked if either tried to snatch at the goodies. When the session ended they were collected and the pair were rewarded with treats that had not been on the ground, those being transferred to a bird table outside the compound.

Once they had learnt that food in the garden was forbidden under all circumstances, each was taken into the woods, where attractive titbits had been put down while the dogs were having the first part of their lesson.

When they refused to touch any food at all unless it was in their bowls and offered by either Lyan or the Colonel, Jan was co-opted, to offer them biscuits from his hands, and scold them if they even tried to take them. It was weeks before the three were satisfied with their teaching. Now, hopefully, they were safe.

Sapphire had completely recovered, and was as frisky

as Quint, racing out into the sunshine, barking suddenly at a bird that flew out of a tree, and flinging herself at Lyan to greet him as if she had not seen him at all that morning.

He realised, as the Colonel came out of the house, that the dogs were therapy. Watching them, he revelled in the heady excitement that filled them with joy, bringing pleasure into his life.

The school lay at the end of the village street, its windows looking out on the church and the distant hill. An old building, it was kept in good condition by villagers who gave their time to ensuring that the roof did not let in the rain, and that the classrooms were clean and brightly painted. There was a strong parents' committee and the village happily attended the fête held each year, to provide welcome money for repairs and extras.

There had been a move to close it some years before but nobody wished small children to travel the dangerous winding roads to Pyneton. Here they were within easy reach of home. Few stayed for lunch, except rarely when a parent was ill or in hospital. Then they brought sandwiches and Miss Carton provided soup as there were never more than a couple at one time.

The class that afternoon was as difficult as Lyan had feared. The wind was still blowing outside. It sped round the corners, producing eerie noises that frightened some of the younger children.

The youngest of them all, Lucy Cartwright's smallest sister, was sure that there were wild animals out there, busy killing things, and refused to be comforted. Miss Carton, who was taking her class, knew better than to ask Lucy to come and help. She suspected that little Belinda was afraid of the older girl.

Lyan had the top class for an English lesson. He had planned meticulously, but began to have doubts as to whether his ideas would work.

He was teaching the importance of using the right words, of the way they could convey emotion—excitement or despair.

He suggested that each child should choose a poem and read it to the class, hopefully illustrating how their selection induced a mood, or provoked happiness or laughter.

He waited with interest to see what they had chosen. Most read badly, their voices toneless, stumbling over the words, having little feeling for what was written.

Some, he suspected, had made their selection to impress him, using poems that he had read to them. Few seemed to have a genuine liking for the piece. They would probably prefer to read from a comic, he thought, wondering if his teaching had any effect at all. Long before the end of the lesson he regretted having read Wordsworth's 'Daffodils' to them, having heard it five times.

Shelley chose Belloc's 'Do you remember an Inn, Miranda?' and read it with love, so that the children sat up, eyes bright, when she came to 'the Hip! Hop! Hap!/ Of the clap/Of the hands to the twirl and the swirl/Of the girl gone dancing . . .'

Her voice deepened and slowed as she came to 'the boom/Of the far Waterfall like Doom.'

He spoke to them for a few minutes, pointing out the way the rhythm changed, how the lines moved fast when the poet wrote of the dancer, and then the slow, sorrowful notes of regret, 'Never more, Miranda, never more.'

That phrase reminded him of Poe's 'The Raven', and he read that to them. 'Quoth the raven, "nevermore"'. Poe, who was not one of his favourite authors, always fascinated his classes and he wondered why children were so morbid. Had they always been?

Mark was looking at him, his small face anxious. He was a delicate child, with enormous brown eyes set in a pallid little face, topped by a thatch of thick golden hair.

His mother called him Thistletop and he prayed nightly that she would never say it in public.

'What poem did you choose, Mark?' Lyan asked.

' "The Runaway", by Robert Frost.'

'Why did you choose that?'

'It's about a colt ... a Morgan. My mother breeds Morgans.' He didn't add that she seemed to like them better than she liked her son, but Lyan picked the thought out of the air and frowned.

'My dad breeds 'ubbards. They 'uddle,' said Lucy Cartwright, grinning all over her little round face as she threw her usual spanner, changing the subject entirely and drawing attention to herself. Lyan felt he ought to stop the interventions, but was curious.

'What's 'ubbards?' asked Davey Prentice.

'Chickens, stupid. Everyone knows that.'

'They always 'uddle,' said Peter Gidd scornfully. His father had a small-holding on which he kept sheep and geese and chickens as well as two donkeys. These were a spare time hobby as he worked for the Electricity Board.

Hubbards, thought Lyan, enlightened. I didn't know they huddled. I wonder why they do?

'Rhode Island Reds is best,' Shelley said. Her parents had a chicken farm. Free range. So for that matter were Jim Cartwright's chickens, even venturing into the woods, and small surprise if a fox did take them.

'Are best,' Lyan said, the correction automatic. Shelley, who had already forgotten what she had said, stared at him in amazement.

Rain rattled against the window panes, and the wind increased its fury, momentarily drowning conversation of any kind. Lyan had intended to ask Mark to read, but Davey was fidgeting, whispering to the child next to him, who giggled. Better get his over first. Goodbye, preparation and plans.

'Davey, what have you brought to read us?'

Something I won't like, Lyan thought, wondering what the boy could find in the way of poetry to give annoyance. He wondered too, not for the first time, if Davey spent his spare time thinking up ways to irritate his teachers.

When he was grown he would look exactly like his father, a tall man, now running to fat, with a large red face that always suffered from five o'clock shadow, and a mat of thick dark hair that was never well cut. Davey was big for his age, towering above little Mark, who was terrified of him and spent his play-time shadowing Lyan hoping to avoid the councillor's son.

There was a smirk on the boy's face that Lyan distrusted. Davie began to read.

'Little Willie in his nice blue sashes
Fell in the fire and was burned to ashes.
The night grew dark and the night grew chilly
But we hadn't the heart to poke poor Willie.'

There was a pause and then a riot of laughter except from Shelley and Mark who both looked horrified.

'I'd 'ave poked him,' Davey said. 'I like fire. Wonder if teeth burn?'

'Where did you find that?' Lyan asked, unable to think of any appropriate comment.

'My dad's *Book of Comic Verse,*' Davey said, holding it up. 'There's lots more like it.'

'There's a difference between verse and poetry.' Lyan wished that he could find something about the boy that he liked. He was becoming paranoid, expecting him to disrupt the lessons. If Davey could create mayhem he did, and pretended astonishment when he discovered that his efforts were not appreciated. The children were all restless now, giggling and murmuring, buzzing with expectancy of further entertainment.

124

'I like limericks,' Davey said, his grin again intended to provoke. 'I wrote one. Can I tell you?'

Lyan hesitated, not at all sure that it was wise to agree, but knowing that his tormentor would dream up even more aggravation if he did not.

'Go ahead.'

> 'There was an old man of Dunbar
> Who was hit in the face with a jar.
> The corner was jagged,
> The cutting was ragged,
> And my word, but you should see the scar!'

Lyan held on to his temper with difficulty, keeping his face as devoid of expression as possible. Lucy and Davey were both watching him, their eyes gleeful, but the other children sat silent, feeling that Davey this time had gone too far.

There was bile in Lyan's throat and he was sure that the scarred side of his face had flamed crimson.

'You seem to have mastered the idea,' he said, refusing to be goaded. He had never known time move so slowly. The unwilling hands on the clock were crawling. He had a double period and he always dreaded it. It was far too long.

'Time for Mark to read his poem.' He couldn't run away. He could do nothing to curb his two persecutors. Perhaps he could distract them. Mark rarely read aloud and when he did had little inflection in his voice and he did not expect to be impressed.

The child began to speak in a low, intense tone that was nothing like his usual high-pitched uncertain treble. He read with passion, silencing his classmates.

> 'And now he comes again with a clatter of stone
> And mounts the wall again with whited eyes
> And all of his tail that isn't hair up straight . . .'

They were out on the hill watching the terrified colt flying through the snow, 'like a shadow against the curtain of falling flakes', alone and uncared-for. Mark ended with anger in his voice.

'Whoever it is that leaves him here so late
When everything else has gone to stall and bin
Ought to be told to go and bring him in.'

'I think that's silly,' said Lucy Cartwright. 'You don't put farm animals indoors; horses can live out in all weathers. Ours do.'

'Yours are Shetlands, bred for bad weather, with heavy winter coats,' Mark said, speaking with confidence about a subject he knew well, surprising Lyan who had never realised the child had so much courage. Mark loved the horses, especially the foals, and the thought of so much terror horrified him. His mother cared for them with great devotion. 'This colt was in America, or maybe Canada. I'm not sure. Anyway, winters there are far worse than ours and nobody would leave him out if they had any sense at all.'

'I suppose your mum puts coats on hers and tucks them up in bed and kisses them goodnight,' Lucy Cartwright said.

Lyan was startled by the flash of fury in Mark's eyes. It was time to change the pattern of their thoughts. He wished he were back in the days when no child dared even speak in class during a lesson. He had a sudden vision of himself asking a question when he ought to have been writing and could almost feel the sharp edge of the ruler that the maths master had brought down on the back of his hand.

'Silence, Grant,' the teacher had roared.

If I did that today I'd be sacked, Lyan thought. How

could anyone run a class well when it contained children like Lucy and Davey?

He wondered whether they even understood what he was saying, though he was sure that little Mark Luton, who was too small for his age and suffered from that, and Shelley Dane did understand. Both had a feeling for language. Mark had produced a poem, the week before, that provoked pity when Lyan read it:

> I walk like a shadow.
> No one sees me.
> When I come home
> No one is there
> To say
>   'Hello. How are you?
>   Did you have a good day?'
> No kisses.
> No hugs.
> When they come home they say
>   'Hang up your coat.
>   Do your homework.
>   Don't chatter. We're tired.'
> I think I'm invisible.
> I wish I had a cat.
> I could cuddle that.

Lyan felt a sudden wave of anger against the parents who left their small son to his own devices and seemed to have no time for him. It brought back his own hunger. Did his ex-wife and her new man treat his children like that? He would have liked to hug the child himself, give him some human contact, but that was impossible as his motives would at once be suspect if anyone reported him. The villagers could summon scandal out of nowhere.

He remembered crying at school because his dog had

been run over. He had been six years old and the head-master had held him on his lap and mopped up the tears and comforted him. If he were to do that now . . . damn this modern attitude, he thought, often seeing misdoing where none exists.

The dusty classroom was claustrophobic, smelling of children and chalk and an indescribable mixture of other odours. One small girl had stolen her mother's perfume and sprayed it lavishly, causing the child next to her to cough. Lyan, listening, prayed that this was not one who was likely to have an asthma attack. He longed for the wind in the trees and the shelter of the woods and to see Silver stepping regally across the glade.

Davey had made an aeroplane out of a sheet of paper. He aimed it at Lyan, who caught it without comment and put it in the waste-paper basket. He thought it was a mercy that there were no longer ink-wells or there would be blotting paper soaked in ink flicked across the room from rubber bands. Thank heaven for ballpoint pens.

The fidgeting was worse than ever. Davey was whisper-ing, Lucy was flicking paper pellets at the child in front of her, who was becoming tearful, and total disruption threatened unless he could recapture their interest. What did interest them? He glanced out of the window. There was a bonfire burning in the garden of the house across the road.

Time to abandon his preconceived plan for the lesson.

'Let's think about words associated with fire and fire-works.' He hoped that the mere thought of such excite-ments might start imaginations working. These children were ten- and eleven-year-olds and some were very cap-able, so long as their interest was aroused.

'Flash,' said a child at the back of the class.

'Flame, flare,' said another.

'Flicker,' Lucy Cartwright said, surprising her teacher, as she rarely contributed.

'They're all F-words,' said Davey Prentice, provoking a giggle that spread round the room.

Lyan decided to ignore him.

'What about blaze and bang and crash and shooting stars, and streams of light, and glitter and sparkle and gleam and glow? Anyone want to try and make a poem about them?'

He glanced at his watch.

'Four lines. Five minutes.'

Most of the children seemed unable to think of anything at all, but several pens wrote busily. Mark wrote:

> The night
> Is bright
> With sparkling light
> For my delight.

Lucy surprised him with her four lines:

> Flare and flicker
> Flame and flash
> Sparking light
> And thunder crash.

'You mean sparkling,' Davey said.

'I don't. I mean sparking ... sparks, stupid.' She grinned at Lyan. 'I like fireworks. Especially Roman candles. Our barn caught fire and the firemen came. Wonderful flames shooting up into the night.'

Lyan looked at her uneasily, wondering if she had started the blaze.

The clanging bell released him. He collected the previous day's homework.

He had asked the children to write about Staghill and what it meant to all of them. Davey Prentice, handing in his, looked at him, a smug smile on his lips and an odd expression in his eyes. Lyan wondered about it and wondered about it again that evening when he began to correct the class work.

Staghill, it was obvious, meant little to most of them. A place to walk and pick snowdrops and primroses in the spring, a hill beyond the village where some were not allowed to wander. He read and reread Lucy's and Davey's contributions with increasing unease.

Lucy had written:

Staghill is where the witch lives. The fudge lady says she ought to be drummed out, as witches are wicked people and when the fox got our chickens my dad said it was her folt because she gave him food and made him come to the hill. She does spells and walks in the wood at night and the ghost stag walks behind her and Doomsday Tom says it means she'll die soon. Then we wont have a witch to worry about. My mum wont let me go up there in case she puts a spell on me. Dad says there was a witch there long ago. All witches rot in hell because they are very bad people. They arent human. They are probably aliens from Mars. The witch woman came with the old man from Africa where they have witch doctors and the fudge lady says they taught her to be wicked. She says she looks after sick animals and makes them well, but really they are all sacrifices and buried in her garden. Lots of them. I bet she was the one that poisoned our cat and the dog at the Place. The fudge lady says the sooner she's gone the better and the old man who isn't really her grandfather though he says he is which she says is wicked too, then Staghill will be free from wickedness again. They burned witches at the steak, she says. I wonder if they smelled like burnt chicken? One got burnt in our barn when it was on fire.

Lyan read it through again, absentmindedly correcting the spelling and punctuation, worrying about the prejudice in the village and the fact that it was affecting the children. While adults might do nothing about the situation, children might think it a good idea to try to drive the intruders away. Were Lucy and Davey responsible for those letters? And who was laying poison?

He sighed as he opened Davey's badly written offering. Spelling seemed beyond his capability.

There used to be a wich in the old cottage and there is again. She makes spells and only goes out at nite becos wiches dont like daylite. She puts spells on the cows and sheep and they dye. She lives with an old man. Lucy and me walk on Staghill and we mete this nice old lady who gives us cakes and fudge and she says wiches ort to be burned. She says we dont want strangers in the village. They all ort to go back where they belong.

Lyan sat, shaking with anger. He wondered who on earth it was that the pair met, who was feeding them such stories. Somehow he would have to talk to the children, maybe even show them the film of Torran with the animals, and change their minds.

Sapphire scratched at his door and he let her in.

'Oh girl, girl,' he said, as he rubbed her ears. 'What the hell are we going to do?'

The bitch, unnerved by anger that was almost palpable, butted his knee, looking into his face as if afraid she were the cause. Lyan picked up the two exercise books and went downstairs for his evening meal, wondering whether or not to show them to the Colonel. Surely the children would never go beyond thinking about doing harm?

Twelve

Sapphire bounded down the stairs, racing to Quint to greet him as if they had not seen one another for weeks. The two dogs, elated, rolled over, embracing, growling in pretended anger and mouthing one another.

'That's enough,' the Colonel said, and, abashed, knowing that play indoors was forbidden, they settled side by side, their expressions meek, good dogs who would never dream of misbehaving. The Colonel laughed and then looked up as Lyan came into the room. His expression changed.

'When I was a boy,' he said, 'there were five of us. My father was a morose man with a ready temper and we evolved a system. If there was a black ribbon lying on the hall table when we came in then it was "Watch out. Dad's in one of his moods", and we tiptoed carefully all evening. You are producing the same atmosphere. Bad day?'

Lyan made a wry face.

'My mother was our problem,' he said. 'We never knew whether her blood was boiling or her marrow was freezing, and so many things could produce either result.' He stopped to think about the matter in hand. 'Whatever it was, it meant a bad evening. I'm sorry. Just had a lousy day. The children were worse than usual. I dread wind. It seems to make them crazy.'

He decided not to worry the Colonel. The two essays were childish nonsense, and meant nothing. Davey and Lucy were punishing him for championing Torran when they were chanting at her in the woods. They had been listening to adults talking. He hoped the stories were not widespread. He also hoped that he was worrying without cause.

He sighed and settled in one of the large leather armchairs that had replaced Miss Stephanie's delicate chintzy antiques. They too had sold for a price that the Colonel found difficult to believe, although Melissa had told him they were sought-after items.

This was the only room the Colonel had altered. Bookshelves filled with thick volumes of military history covered two walls. The flowery curtains had been replaced by heavy drapes. The windows were large and in winter the room was very cold, heated only by the coal fire.

Central heating was confined to the kitchen, the sitting-room and Mrs Burton's two rooms, as the cost of warming the whole house would have been prohibitive. The Victorian pictures that Miss Stephanie had loved had also been consigned to one of the weekly auction sales in Pyneton, fetching very little. Few people wanted such themes now. They were poor reprints in ugly frames.

In their place were stormy seas, waves crashing against rocks, elemental fury in all of them. Lyan felt a longing to walk on a wintry beach, the white spume flying on the air and pounding against the cliffs, birds fighting against the storm. He loved the suck and swirl of the racing tide as the waves receded down the shingle.

The Colonel glanced at his watch.

'Mrs B's late. That's not like her.'

Dorothy Burton's days were dominated by the clock. She washed the kitchen floor at eleven each morning. Breakfast was served at seven forty-five; lunch at twelve forty-five; and the evening meal at six forty-five. Neither man dared be late. Her wrath was immediate if anyone disrupted her routine.

Even the arrival of a dog in the kitchen at the wrong time was enough to provoke her. Sapphire had learnt never to transgress but Quint was a total extrovert who could never understand anyone who rejected his overtures. He reminded Lyan of Bobby Leigh, a charming child with learning difficulties, who could never understand what he had done wrong.

When the housekeeper's orderly life was interrupted her sniffs became frequent, and the atmosphere she generated worried the bitch. If Sapphire looked haunted, the men knew they were about to suffer a stormy day.

The door slammed open, hitting the wall. The housekeeper erupted into the room. She wore a white nylon overall over the calf-length skirt and matching hand-knitted twin set that seemed almost to be a uniform. She was never seen in any colour other than black, grey or brown. She banged the tray on to the table and slammed the plates into each place. Her colour was high and she seemed to have difficulty in speaking.

'Jim Cartwright was here. Making a scene. I stopped him coming in. It's bad enough to have the food ruined without him preventing you from eating it while it's hot.'

The Colonel glanced at the clock. They had been waiting for over ten minutes. Such tardiness was unprecedented.

'It doesn't look ruined to me,' he said, eyeing his plateful of steak, creamed potatoes and carrots with appreciation. The sauce, he was sure, would be as good as the food looked.

'He was angry. He was drunk. He says your dogs have been worrying his sheep. There's two dead and nine injured, and he's telling the police.'

'The dogs . . .' The Colonel began to speak, but was swiftly interrupted.

'I warned you. German Shepherds are never safe. Treacherous beasts, and sheep killing's in their blood. I've seen Quint look at the birds . . . if he could catch them he'd kill them. Both ought to be put down.'

The Colonel put his hand on Quint's neck. The dog

134

was growling under his breath and his ruff was bristling. Sapphire had retreated and was lying out of sight, behind Lyan's chair.

Dorothy Burton looked at the two men, her eyes bright, enjoying the effect she was having on them.

'It only takes a minute for them to run down the hill to the farm. Jim's quite sure it was your two dogs. He saw them. He shot at them, but missed.'

The Colonel was so angry he banged his fist on the table to quieten her.

'Hold your tongue, woman! Neither dog has left my side for weeks and well you know it. You could have quashed that story at once, instead of allowing him to go away believing it. He's probably now in the village accusing my dogs when others are to blame.'

He looked at his plate, his appetite gone. He couldn't bear her presence in the room and wished she would go.

'You've lived with the dogs for long enough. You know perfectly well neither of them has ever harmed any other animal. Quint brings live hedgehogs and Sapphire can pick up a fledgling bird that's fallen from the nest and bring it back without a mark on it. If you don't like the dogs . . .'

Dorothy Burton stared at him, realising she had gone too far. She sniffed, and walked out of the room, shutting the door behind her so carefully that she might as well have slammed it.

'Jim's out of his mind,' the Colonel said. 'Does he suppose I'll let him keep on the tenancy of the farm if he reports the dogs for something they have never done. Suppose they believe him and not me?'

The thought of losing the dogs was unbearable.

'He was drunk,' Lyan said. Lucy had written a short essay about dogs worrying the sheep, but had said they were village dogs. Not everyone was as careful as they were to see that their pets never wandered. He often met the blacksmith's terrier foraging alone in the woods, and worried lest it harm the wild animals.

Both men made a pretence of eating. The steak was overdone and the sauce had a most peculiar flavour. The two dogs, to their delight, found themselves given more than half of each man's meal.

'I don't approve,' the Colonel said, a smile on his lips as he watched Quint sit and lick his chops, an expression of bliss on his face. The dogs did not have table scraps, although they were sometimes rewarded with small left-overs from each man's plate. 'She meant to upset us. She never has liked the dogs. I don't want her to know she succeeded.'

'Maybe we should go and see Jim?' Lyan was not sure that that would do any good. There was nothing worse than a drunken man with a fixed idea. Nothing would change his mind. Drunks also resorted to violence. Jim was unpredictable.

'I don't know.' The Colonel frowned. 'It might be better to wait until the morning. There's a story round the village that he spends more time drunk than sober. He's no longer welcome at the Dog and Duck. He's caused problems.'

Lyan thought of Jim's children, and the woman who had to cope with his excesses. Perhaps that accounted for Lucy's naughtiness and Belinda's fearfulness. He felt helpless.

'We need to take the dogs out. We can go down towards the farm. A walk will do us all good. Maybe we'll meet him . . . let's leave it to chance. I don't want to confront him. If we call at his home, it will look as if I intend to do just that.'

It seemed sensible. Lyan, following the Colonel through the front door, wished that there were more smooth passages in life.

Sapphire and Quint were leashed. The Colonel had no

intention of letting them run ahead. If Jim saw them he might be so provoked that he shot them. It only took a moment . . .

A small wind whispered in the branches. The dogs were eager, as usually at this time their exercise was confined to a run round the garden. Here there were wonderful scents on the ground, that told of the passage of fox or badger, and the rustles in the bushes held promise. They resented the lack of freedom and both tugged at their leads.

Higher on the hill the badger boar smelled the dogs and retreated to his sett. The sow guarded her family as footsteps vibrated on the ground. The deer, smelling man, sought sanctuary. Silver, on his way to the cottage, looking for Torran, hid in deep cover, ready to run.

The dogs were aware of the hidden animals, catching a scent in the air, or a sound on the wind. They longed to be free to explore.

'No one would think we had ever trained them.' The Colonel was exasperated. The quiet and relaxed stroll he had envisaged had become a battle between wayward dogs and weary men.

The ten-minute walk along the path to the village intensified the dogs' feelings. They were rarely taken far in the dark and both were wary, their protective instincts intensified. Sapphire shied as they passed a small rhododendron that seemed to reach out to trap her. The moving branches were threats.

The wind sighed in the trees, a background to the murmur of running water from the brook that tumbled over loose rocks.

It was now shallow, a deceptive appearance as rain and wind could rouse it to a raging torrent, surging with a violence that crashed the boulders as the peaty water thundered on its way to the river which it fed.

Lyan had only once seen it in spate. He was awed by the

ferocity of the seething water and the deafening rumble of the huge stones that were tossed as if they were pebbles. Neither man nor beast could survive if they fell in.

Tonight it was a glinting streak between the banks. There were otters, but neither man had seen them, though the dogs knew that they had passed.

They walked through the tiny alleyway that led to the village street, the dogs almost dancing in their pleasure at being part of this foray. Light shone from the vicarage windows and from the church where the organist was practising. They paused to listen, as the deep notes swelled on the air.

Light patched the cottages and spilled from the doorway of the Dog and Duck as it was flung open and someone went inside.

'Care to go in?' Roger asked.

'Don't feel sociable,' Lyan said. 'Don't let me stop you.'

'Might as well get back. The dogs would be bored anyway and we did come out for their benefit.'

They took the footpath that led through fields at the back of the village, saying nothing, both busy with their own thoughts. Quint and Sapphire were kept at heel, although unleashed. They had spent much of their energy and could be trusted to walk soberly home, though the Colonel was ready to leash them at once at the slightest sound. Even a trained dog might be tempted if cat or fox or badger appeared on the path. He was afraid of another poisoning episode.

They were halfway up the lane that led to the Place when Sapphire growled, almost under her breath, and Quint stiffened, his head going up. A twig snapped, some way above them. Someone coughed softly, trying to stifle the sound.

'Poachers on the hill,' the Colonel whispered, quietening the dogs and leashing them. 'Take Sapphire and see

138

if you can find them. I'll go back with Quint and get Matt. She won't bark; Quint might forget himself.'

Lyan slipped between the trees, thankful for his knowledge of the woods. He knew the fox and badger trails, as well as the deer paths, beaten out down the centuries by animals that followed their own ways and learned them from their mothers.

An owl floated between the trees and, far away, another hooted and was answered. Sapphire nosed a tuft of grass, scenting mouse, but the little animal had passed an hour before and she found nothing.

Lyan climbed, keeping the bitch close beside him. She was wary, her ears moving constantly, as she caught sounds that were inaudible to the man. He was spurred into action when, from above, came a noisy barking and men yelling to encourage their dogs.

'Get her, lads, good lads, go on then. Kill! Kill! Kill!'

Lyan put his hand over Sapphire's mouth, to stifle any desire to respond to the sounds.

'Quiet, girl. Good girl. Let's go,' he whispered, and ran with her bounding beside him, aware that there was danger on the hill.

Thirteen

The cat had increasingly been having problems with her small family and had also begun to distance herself from the cubs, although as yet she still helped them hunt.

Ric was always first out of the den and last in, usually driven there by his frantic foster-mother. He loved the darkness and was fascinated by the moon, often staring up at it, as if trying to work out why it was there and what it did. He was staring at it the night that the dogs returned, hidden behind a hollow tree that had fallen in the recent storms. His sister and two brothers were playing in a little glade, teasing and chasing, fighting mock battles. They were heady with youth, forgetful of danger, absorbed in their games.

The cat was hunting. She heard the agonised squeal as the little vixen died. The terriers were worrying the second cub when Nemesis dropped on them from the tree above. She was swift and she was defending her family. Her raking claws slashed viciously and drew blood time and again, and her teeth bit.

She was faster than the Jack Russells, leaping away from them, then racing in to deliver another savage slash, cutting deep. The woods reverberated with the shouts of the men trying to draw her off, with the squeals of the injured dogs and the high, screaming fury of the cat as she drew away to rally her wits before launching herself again.

Mother instinct gave her immense strength and the terriers had no chance. One of them, escaping from her as she defended the two brothers, found Ric and attacked him. He resisted, biting and snapping, but was not big enough to overcome his enemy. His foster-mother, having driven away one opponent, flew to his rescue, landing on the dog's back.

She clung, claws anchoring, driving deep into his flesh, while she bit his ear and he screamed with pain. He twisted and she rolled, slashing upwards with her hind claws, which dug into his defenceless belly, delivering wounds that were, in a few days' time, to prove fatal.

He fled.

The men tried to deter her, thrashing at her with their sticks, but were unable to touch the quicksilver body. One reached down to his dog, intending to lift him by his scruff, and suffered for his stupidity. He withdrew, his finger bitten to the bone. He swore, angrily and continuously.

The second terrier raced off, whimpering. He was very badly mauled, and even his immense courage was defeated by the wildness of his opponent and her extra armoury. He, unlike his companion, survived, but never tackled any other animal again. His owner, infuriated by his cowardice, shot him.

Torran had been below them when she heard the sounds of fighting. She saw the dogs fly past her. She heard the shriek as another of the cubs died, his life ended by a blow from the heavy cudgel.

She raced up the hill and ran at the men, forgetting her fear in her anxiety for the animals. She shouted at them.

'Don't you dare come here again with those dogs.' They stared at her, an avenging angel, coming out of the night. One laughed, and put out a hand to grab at her. The next moment he yelled as teeth sank deep into his leg.

Amber, who was now a shadow following her rescuer wherever she went, had flown to protect her new mistress.

Lyan was appalled when he saw Torran run towards the source of the outcry. He had noticed the van as he sped up the hill, parked off the track, almost in the bushes, and knew that the men might have no more respect for her than they had for the foxes.

Moonlight betrayed them. They had sticks, not guns. terrier men, out for fun, not poachers. Both men were younger than he and probably fitter. He slipped behind the second man, thrusting the thick stick he had just picked up into the small of his back. He prayed that the intruder would not realise the ruse.

As the second man moved Sapphire leaped to the end of her lead, barking her fury.

'Move, and I let her go,' Lyan said, praying his bluff was not called. He was not sure if Sapphire would protect him. That was a discipline they had not taught, feeling it unwise with pet dogs. Any attack might invoke the law, even if it had been provoked. The man stood still, daunted by the authority in Lyan's voice.

'Now, down the hill, both of you, Any bother, and I'll release the dog.' Sapphire, barking and straining at her lead, gave an impression of immense fury.

Lyan thought he saw a movement in the trees and prayed that no third man was there, as he would be sure to see that Lyan held a stick and not a gun. No one came forward and he relaxed. Maybe the third man had thought it wiser to vanish.

He did not realise that Silver was watching from a safe distance, with Missie, whom he had nudged into hiding, beside him. The dogs fled beneath the van, where they lay miserably licking one another's injuries. They had not caught the deer scent, nor were they in any shape to pursue another quarry.

Clouds were drifting across the moon. Lyan tensed as three figures walked up the path towards him, and then relaxed again as he saw Quint. He was glad to surrender his captives to the two policemen, Matt having called up reinforcements. He handed Sapphire's leash to the Colonel and sped back up the hill.

Torran was kneeling beside the cat. She had been badly injured and lay, exhausted, spitting weakly. The little vixen and one of her brothers was dead. Ric was severely bitten and the other cub died as Lyan bent over him.

'I could kill them.' Torran was beginning to shake. 'What kind of men are they?'

He looked down at the cat and the cub.

'Could you carry the cub in your anorak? Watch he doesn't bite. My coat will keep me safe from this one, but I think she's too weak at present to resist.'

The cat was drifting in a sea of pain. She was terrified of the man who lifted her, associating him with those who had urged the dogs to harm her, but she had lost all strength. She could not challenge.

Lyan examined her carefully, watchful of claws and teeth, but she did not even lift her head.

'She's bitten and torn, but all the injuries are on her legs or back; had they caught her underneath . . .' He did not need to elaborate.

Ric produced a feeble hiss. He was exhausted and had never known such agony. He had bites on his shoulder and all four legs, as well as a badly torn cheek, just below his right eye.

Torran wrapped him gently in her anorak, fighting tears. Both animals were covered in blood and it was difficult to see the full extent of their wounds. She hoped that they looked worse than they actually were.

The cub struggled feebly, disliking the clinging cloth and the strange smells that overwhelmed him. The hand that held him touched lightly, but still confined him, and he gave up, too frightened and weary to try to wriggle free.

Lyan had nothing to say. He felt that he had failed. He should have realised that the little family was vulnerable and watched over them with more care.

Peace had gone from Staghill. He wondered if it would

ever return. The outside world was thrusting itself upon him wherever he went and there was no escape.

' "The woods are lovely, dark and deep",' Torran said, but her voice was forlorn. 'I'll never think that again. I'm not sure I'll even dare come out at night now. They'll be back . . . and Silver and the other deer are at risk.'

'We'll watch for the vans. There are only two places where they can park. There are others who'll join in. There's a flourishing badger watch group in Pyneton, who are protecting the animals against just this sort of thing. I'll involve them.'

It was a small comfort, but Torran was not sure that anyone could keep away the intruders.

The woodland path was steep and the moon gave very little light. Clouds drifted across remote stars. It was essential to watch the ground, which was rutted and strewn with tumbled rocks.

Behind them Silver positioned himself at Torran's shoulder and the little spaniel hugged her ankles, so close that she almost tripped her owner. A small shape slipped out of the darkness as Missie joined them. She had been terrified by the din above her. Silver knew that, if they ran, they might well be chased and caught, and had forced her to lie as still as, when a baby, her mother had hidden her in deep bracken.

In spite of all that had happened, Lyan felt a sudden elation. The animals had never trusted him before. He wondered what sort of picture they made coming down the hill. Better than the Pied Piper. He hated rats.

'People haven't really changed.' Torran eased the cub onto her other arm. He was frozen with terror, lying quite still, unable to understand what was happening to him. The voices bothered him, as did the smell of the deer and the dog. He could smell the cat and knew she was near and that gave him some comfort.

'In Africa . . . here . . . they haven't ever become really

civilised. I feel eyes in the woods, watching me . . . in the past few weeks I've felt more and more on edge.'

She sighed.

'Maybe they were watching the animals, not me, planning to kill. Poor little cat . . . judging by the weight of this little fellow she's done a terrific job in bringing him up. I wonder what made her adopt them?'

'She probably lost her own litter and found these just when they were needing her and she needed young to feed. I've known cats bring up the oddest animals—rabbits, ferrets, puppies—when their own kittens died.'

'We had a bitch in Africa who adopted a baby monkey. He used to ride on her back.'

The pang of memory stung her, and she swallowed, trying not to give way to tears. The cub whimpered, pain overwhelming him, and Torran was suddenly so angry that she could not prevent herself from shouting her rage.

'I won't let them die!'

It was a challenge to God, to fate, to whatever ruled the lives of the creatures that roamed the earth, including man.

They stopped at the edge of a clearing. Lyan was afraid that the cat had died. She was so still. He wanted to look at her, but without worrying Torran still more, in case he was wrong.

'I hope this poor animal can breathe,' he said. 'I need to loosen my coat and make sure.'

Torran leaned against a tree, shifting the cub from one arm to the other. He hissed again, a feeble sound that carried only the reminder of a threat. His head was free, and he smelled the woodland air, savouring familiar scents. The old badger was abroad and not far away. They heard his ponderous tread and a sudden grunt as he trod on a thorny twig that hurt his pad. There were pheasants roosting in the trees and the scent of mouse was strong on a needling wind that reminded both Lyan and Torran that they had shed their outer wear.

Lyan opened his coat and shone the torch on the cat. She was almost unconscious and seemed to be barely breathing, but there was a slight rise and fall of her chest and one paw twitched.

'She's not dead?'

'Not yet. We need to hurry if we're going to save her.'

They were on the lower slopes where the path was level and wide, allowing them to increase their speed. Lyan recognised that he was now an ally and was trusted. Time was an enemy to be fought if the cat were to survive. He thought that the cub was more likely to recover.

There was no breath now for talk. Torran was praying inside her head, praying to the God of her childhood, praying that this time He would hear.

Please, don't let her die.

She felt the faint struggles of the cub in her arms and was thankful: it was a sign of his own will to survive. They reached the cottage clearing and Missie and Silver and Amber left them, seeking shelter in their shed, still unnerved by the events of the night.

Jan and the Colonel were waiting for them when they arrived at the door. Roger, seeing that both were safe, returned with the dogs to his own home. Lyan laid the little cat on the hearthrug. She looked very near to death. Torran put Ric beside her.

The cub nosed his foster-mother anxiously, needing comfort. He cuddled against her, pushing her with his head, trying to gain her attention.

'Would Angus come here?' Torran asked, hoping that Lyan knew the answer. 'We can't stress them any more tonight and a journey to the surgery would be an immense ordeal for both of them.' Angus was the new young vet. Mac no longer took night calls.

Jan was already dialling. He explained the situation.

'He'll come,' he said. 'But if either needs an operation he'll have to take them back with him. He can sedate them. We can't.'

Light from the window shone into the garden, illuminating the shelter where the deer and the spaniel were cuddled together in the straw. Amber preferred to be outside, but was instantly at Torran's heels when she walked in the woods.

Jan made coffee laced with whisky. Torran, white-faced, sat, wondering at her own temerity. She was now far more frightened than she had been when she approached the men. Lyan, exhausted by the evening's events, stared sombrely at the two animals. Both needed their wounds cleaning, but maybe it was better to let them lie still, undisturbed, rather than subject them to human touch again.

'Did you know she'd adopted the cubs?' Torran asked, wondering, as she looked down at the two unlikely companions. They both looked very near to death. Hatred filled her, wishing every ill she could think of on their attackers.

'I've filmed her. You've been very elusive these last few weeks, otherwise I would have told you.'

Amber barked as Angus's Land-Rover parked outside the cottage. Lyan had not met him before. He saw a long-legged young man with a thatch of tousled dark hair badly in need of cutting. Brown eyes became angry as he saw his patients.

'I can look after them if you can deal with them here.' Torran had a passionate need to help heal them both.

'I'll sedate them both, and then have a good look. Hopefully there's nothing that a few stitches and antibiotics won't cure.'

The cub snapped and tried to bite as the needle went in. The cat made a small moaning sound.

'Takes about ten minutes,' Angus said, gratefully

accepting the hot coffee that Jan presented to him.

Lyan sat, drained of all energy, while Angus bathed the bites and stitched them. His deft hands were competent and Lyan remembered Effie's strictures and wondered if she now accepted the new vet. Her ginger cat was, he knew, her adored companion.

As if reading the other man's thoughts, Angus tidied up his instruments and then spoke.

'Effie Green's lost her cat,' he said. 'He went out last night and hasn't come back, which is most unusual. He's neutered and never out at night, even in high summer when some cats do refuse to come in. She's distraught, and terrified that someone has run him over and buried the evidence. It's unbearable when they just vanish. Can you keep a look-out?'

'I'll take Quint tomorrow,' Lyan said. 'He has a wonderful nose and if the cat's lying somewhere injured, he'll soon find him. He could have met with one of the wild cats and lost a fight.'

Or met with the poachers and been killed for fun; or maybe he's been hunting Jim Cartwright's chickens and stopped a load of shot. Lyan tried to distract his thoughts, but found himself wondering how he had ever imagined that the woods were peaceful, a healing sanctuary. There was violence in the hunting hawk, in the swooping owl, in the feral cats, bringing destruction; in the foxes, preying to feed themselves.

Yet at least that was natural, unlike the men who came and killed for the sheer hell of it and derived enjoyment as the animals screamed in agony and died.

'We need a plan,' Angus Moray said, as he walked towards the front door, which opened out of the cottage sitting-room.

The other three in the room looked at him, their faces blank.

'Matt can't manage to keep this place free of intruders

by himself. Maybe if several of us patrol, especially if we have dogs with us, we can prevent more trouble. It's easy to call up reinforcements with a mobile phone and they do work in this area. Mine is a godsend; saves me a lot of unnecessary journeys.'

He thrust a hand through his hair, making it even more untidy.

'Keep those two warm. I'll come up and see them tomorrow. You may have a job persuading them to eat at first, as they'll be very traumatised by their new surroundings. I've a big cage in the van. Mac thought it might be useful. I didn't bring it in, in case I needed to take them back with me. That might still be necessary. We'll see. Some of those bites are very deep and infection could still set in. I may not have used the right antibiotics. Or what I've given them may not suit them. We can't work miracles, even today with all our modern methods.'

Lyan helped bring the cage in, and then went outside again and watched the rear lights vanish into the distance. By the time he returned Torran had covered the base with a thick old blanket and lifted the two inert bodies inside. She looked at them anxiously.

'Do you think they'll survive?'

'Who can tell?'

At least they were still breathing, but the image of the two unmoving bodies haunted him as he walked back to the Place, and he wondered if either would live until morning.

Fourteen

The sun was a glowing hint on the horizon, the sky holding a ghost moon and a few faint stars. The night before was a bad dream. The woods were still, the animals hiding, memory vivid of barking and shouting and dying screams. All would be more wary now, and the sound of a human footstep would send them scurrying into shelter. Lyan knew that it would be weeks before he was able to film any of them again.

He had returned to sleep only briefly, his mind too full of horror. He was thankful when dawn came. He bathed and shaved and dressed, and stood, looking out of the window at a view that never failed to soothe him. The trees were green against a sky that was steadily becoming bluer, faint clouds in the distance teasing one another as they were chased by the wind. The foothills were soft shapes rising towards the higher hidden mountains. The track led down to the stile and beyond it, again hidden by woodland, was Jim Cartwright's farm.

The dogs now always slept in the Colonel's room. Lyan did not want to disturb them, though he would have liked to have the pair beside him, watching their reactions to the scents on the wind and the smells on the ground. He wondered how the cub and the cat had fared during the night, but it was too early to call and ask.

Too early to go in to the school, even though he would be able to busy himself. It was only just after six o'clock. It was milking time at the Cartwright farm and there should be the sounds of lowing cows, of the pumping machines and Alison calling to Will across the yard.

Will, who had left school two years ago at sixteen to help with the cattle, was a tow-haired slender boy with a mischievous glint in his eyes and a merry smile. Of all the family he was the best when it came to dealing with Lucy.

They must have overslept this morning, Lyan thought, as he climbed the stile and dropped on to the path below. The cows were in the Ten Acre. They should have been in the milking parlour. He glanced at his watch.

The terrified yell startled him, and he ran towards the sound, vaulting the gate and arriving at the kitchen door as Lucy burst from it, still screaming. Behind her, in the shadow of the passage beyond the lighted kitchen, Lyan could see Will and his mother standing silent, as if they could not bear to contemplate the sight before them.

Jim Cartwright was stretched on the passage floor, a blanket over him, but it was very clear that he was dead and had been for some hours.

'He came home drunk,' Will said. 'He fell on the floor. It's happened before, often. We couldn't move him. He's too heavy. We did what we always do: put a cushion under his head and a rug over him and left him. He was talking, after a fashion, when we left him.'

'He was singing,' Alison said, as if she couldn't believe it. 'He was singing "Danny Boy". I thought he'd never stop and suddenly he did.'

'He must have tried to get up and fallen again,' Will said, 'That's not where we left him. He was at the foot of the stairs.'

Lyan felt as if he had been pitchforked back into his former occupation. He had never grown used to death. Lucy stared down at her father.

'It's the witch,' she shouted. 'She put a spell on him. She's cursed all of us . . . nothing but bad luck since she came.'

'Shut up, Luce,' Will said, goaded beyond endurance. He wanted to shake her. He was saved from any further need to speak by the sound of the doctor's car coming up the lane.

Jason Hall ducked his head as he came into the passage. He was well over six feet in height and often wished the village homes were loftier. He invariably bumped his head on Effie's kitchen lintel. He knelt beside the farmer.

'Need an inquest, I'm afraid,' he said. 'Not seen him for months. Have to tell the coroner, and the police.'

He sat back on his heels and looked at them, reminding Lyan of a friendly bear with his shaggy hair and beard merging. He was rumpled and untidy, having dressed in a hurry after a brief sleep due to a baby that had decided to arrive in the night.

'Nothing to worry about,' he said, seeing Alison's appalled expression. 'Overweight by about five stone, and drinking himself stupid every night; it's been waiting for him, I'm afraid. Probably a massive stroke, but the post mortem will prove that.'

'Got to do the milking,' Will said as the persistent lowing penetrated his daze. 'Cows won't wait.'

'Can't we move him?' Alison asked. 'It'll upset the two young ones so to see him. They'll be getting up soon.'

Lyan knew Belinda well. Little Chris was due to start school in the autumn.

'Can I do anything?' he asked, at a complete loss.

'Could you take the children to school? Out of the way? There's the animals to feed ... no one's had breakfast ... I can't think ...' She felt as if someone had hit her on the head and she had lost her wits. She looked round for Will, always her mainstay, but he had gone to milk the cows.

Little Chris was standing in his pyjamas at the top of the stairs.

'What's wrong, Mam?'

'Your dad's been taken ill,' the doctor said. 'We're waiting for an ambulance. Can you dress quickly like a good boy and wake Belinda and tell her to dress too? You're going to school with Lucy today.'

Chris raced off, unable to believe his luck.

'I'd better help them,' Alison said, clutching at normality. She edged round the covered hump on the floor, wishing he had chosen somewhere else to fall and then feeling guilt flood her at such an idea.

Lucy had gone into the cowshed where she was provoking Will almost beyond endurance. The doctor took his mobile phone out of his car and, standing in the yard, began a series of calls.

'Strong sweet tea,' he said going into the kitchen. 'Cereal for the children. I've asked Sister Harrington to come up and help for a bit. Lucy's going to cause more mayhem than is necessary. She's done it before, when Chris fell off the back of the tractor and broke his arm. Jim always was a stupid man. Child should never have been there.'

'How will his wife cope?' Lyan asked. He had had only very brief contacts with Mrs Cartwright, who seemed a shadowy figure.

'Very well. She always manages to excel in a crisis. Jim gave her plenty of practice at that. Her life will be much easier now he's gone.' Jason was listening for footsteps on the stairs, anxious to distract the children when they came down.

'The man was a walking disaster. Look.' He opened the bin that stood by the back door and Lyan raised his eyebrows when he saw that it was more than half-filled with whisky bottles. 'A bottle a day man, our Jim. More than halfway to DTs, but never admitting that he had a major problem.'

The nurse's little car drove slowly up the lane, the gears crunching as it climbed the hill. Lyan gritted his teeth. He watched her clamber out, a small, red-headed woman, over-plump, bustling busily into the kitchen. Lucy raced out of the milking parlour, rushed past the two men and hurried indoors.

'Linda Harrington will soon put her in her place,' the doctor said. 'I'll have a word and then be away. Can you manage the children?'

'It's only Christopher. Belinda and Lucy come to school anyway. He can sit and paint or do puzzles; I'll find something.' Eileen Carton would be delighted to have a small child to comfort and distract. He suspected she might start child-minding when she retired.

He could not face the kitchen and walked into the milking parlour. Will, washing down the rear end of the last cow before fixing the cups, nodded to him.

'You'll be used to Lucy,' he said.

It was a statement, not a question.

'How will you manage?' Lyan did not know what to say. Jim's eldest son looked too young to have so much responsibility.

'Better than we ever have.' Will's voice was bitter, his mouth grim. 'We won't have his tantrums and rages. No more of the damage he caused when he was out of control. All the animals will be better off, as well as us. He thought nothing of taking a belt to us, or thumping Mum. He won't be missed.'

'Why did you never tell anyone?'

'How can you?' Will asked. 'We might not have been believed anyway. Everyone knows young Lucy's a trouble-maker. Anything she says that's true she says by accident. Takes after our Dad. It's rubbed off on the rest of us. The Cartwright kids—can't trust any of them as far as you can throw them. You know the village.'

'Yes,' Lyan said. Something in his voice made Will look up, see his scarred face, and flush.

'I'm sorry . . . I didn't mean . . . I know . . . oh hell!' He looked at Lyan in dismay.

'I'm used to it,' the schoolmaster said, but refrained from adding that that didn't stop him minding very much when anyone referred to his disfigurement.

'It still hurts.'

Lyan wondered at Will's perception. He leaned against the bench. He had the beginning of a thumping headache, and dreaded the coming day. The cows stood placidly, waiting release, while the last dregs of milk flowed. One banged a hoof against the partition.

Faced with sudden death his own problems seemed unimportant. He had never been able to cope with death when he was in the police, always too aware of the chaos it left behind.

She would find life tough with four children to bring up, even if there were enough money to run the place. Many farms belonged to the bank. Were they in debt for feed bills and machinery? He doubted if Jim had had any life insurance or had made provision for a pension. He didn't seem that sort of man.

The Colonel might reduce or even waive the rent if there were problems. Funerals cost money too and not everyone had savings.

Will released the cows into the yard. They walked through the open gate into the field, knowing the drill well. They stood and watched them amble lazily and then begin to graze. The day was darkening, rain clouds building, threatening bad weather later.

'Mum and I have run this almost on our own for the past two years,' Will said. 'Won't be no different . . . just easier without having to bother about him. Maybe Lucy will settle down now. She's an odd kid.'

He frowned suddenly.

'Listen.'

The feeble wailing seemed to come from the field beyond that in which Will had just put the cows. He walked briskly across to a stile in the hedge, Lyan following. The barley was higher than their ankles and they skirted it, coming to a headland covered in scrub and nettles.

'Always wanted to clear that out, but never had time,' Will said. 'It's over here.' he looked down into a patch of rough grass. 'Oh damn him to hell!'

He knelt, producing wire-cutters from a deep pocket.

'Need these for Belinda's sheep. Dad gave her two of the orphan lambs. Neither has any sense. They're always getting caught on wire. I told him not to set snares. It's Effie's cat, isn't it?'

'Probably,' Lyan said. He had never seen the cat but knew it was ginger. The cat lay quietly while Will cut it free.

'Need to go to the vet to get that out,' Will said. 'Can't do it without anaesthetic. I'll ring Effie. She can meet you there. I'll tell the kids to hurry.'

Lyan found himself holding a very forlorn animal that relaxed completely in his arms as if aware that humans meant an end to pain. He hoped the leg would not need to be amputated. The wire had bitten deep as the cat struggled.

'I'll have to check all round the place,' Will said, as they walked back to the farmhouse. 'He's been obsessed by the foxes. Probably more snares around, but I don't know where to look. Our own cats could get trapped in them.'

Even Lucy seemed subdued when she saw the cat.

'That's Miss Green's Cass,' she said, mindful of her mother who disapproved of children calling adults by their first names. There was a police car outside now, and another that Lyan thought might belong to the coroner. Alison straightened Chris's socks, and handed out lunch packs for each child. The little boy's eyes shone with delight when she handed his to him.

Lyan glanced at his watch. Eight-thirty. He seemed to have lived a lifetime since he reached the farm. He had better take the children straight to school. He could have done with some breakfast, and had been intending to return home for the meal.

'Have you eaten?' the nurse asked him, seeing his glance at the table. He shook his head.

'Give Cass to me. I'll give him half an aspirin which will help the pain. Coffee in the pot and toast in the rack. Help yourself.'

He ate and drank fast, aware of the need to get the children away, so that Will and his mother could continue their work. The body would have to be taken for autopsy. The procedures were familiar; there would be a great deal to do for everyone concerned.

'Mac's expecting you. Effie will meet you there,' Will said, putting down the phone. The surgery was on the way to the school, which was only a fifteen-minute walk from the farm.

Animals, thought Lyan, as he followed the children into the lane, were most remarkably long-suffering. The cat licked his hand. Maybe Cass was now numbed with pain and no longer felt it.

Lucy walked ahead, ignoring all of them, busy with her own thoughts, a fact that worried Lyan. Chris held Belinda's hand, and was entranced by the thought of going to school long before he should have started.

'Tomorrow,' he said confidently, 'I'll be able to read and do sums like Belinda.' He skipped across the pavement, as they had just reached the village street.

'Mustn't walk on lines,' he said, and concentrated hard to avoid such a disaster. Lyan wondered what he imagined would happen if he did transgress. It seemed a remarkable worry. He had a vague recollection of a poem about lines and squares; something to do with bears, but the memory eluded him.

Effie met them at the surgery door. Lyan's thoughts seemed to be out of control because as she swooped he suddenly thought, 'The Assyrians came down like a wolf on the fold', and where the devil did that come from?

'My poor old boy. How terrible.' She stared in dismay at the injured leg, but relaxed a little as the cat nosed her, greeting her with affection. Tears were running down the over-rouged cheeks.

On another occasion she might have upbraided the children for the father's crime, but Will had rung her, told her they had found her cat, and also what had happened. It would soon be common knowledge in the village if Effie knew, and would save having to spread the news themselves.

He had told Mac too; somehow it made it less traumatic to talk about it, even if hiding half the real facts. Jim had died suddenly, probably of a stroke. No need to say he had been so drunk he couldn't stand; everyone probably knew that anyway.

It was as well that Effie was occupied with the cat, Lyan thought. Otherwise she might have tried to commiserate with the children, and heaven knew how they would react to that. Mac, coming to the door, threw one glance at the schoolmaster and the two little ones standing beside him, and took Cass from Effie, knowing that she would follow him inside.

He glanced at the leg.

'No problem,' he told Belinda and Chris who were watching him anxiously. 'Cass will be as right as ninepence in a few days.' He closed the door firmly and Lyan walked on up the street. Christopher, suddenly overcome at the thought of all those children, slipped his hand into the schoolmaster's.

'Why is ninepence right?' he asked.

Lyan, contemplating the odd phrase, found he had no idea. They had reached the school gates, which absolved him of the need to answer, as Christopher was distracted by the sight of all the children in the playground.

The nurse had rung Miss Carton, who was already waiting for them. Lucy, seeing Davey Prentice, joined him. Belinda was hailed by two girls in her class. Christopher's grip tightened. He suddenly felt very small.

'Come and see our little refuge,' Lyan said. 'Children don't usually come in here, but as it's a very special day for you, you can have the honour of being the only child that ever set foot in the staff room.' He wondered whether to tell the child that his father was dead, but decided to leave that problem to his mother.

Christopher wasn't at all sure what the schoolmaster was talking about, but followed him into the tiny sanctum where Miss Carton had set out a glass of orange juice and a jammy face biscuit, hastily bought from the post office, where Gracie Lea clucked over the news.

'Not surprised, mind,' she said, offering suggestions as to what might console a small boy suddenly pitchforked into such appalling events.

Miss Carton started the smaller children on plasticine modelling which she thought would entertain their unexpected pupil. He was daunted by his surroundings and sat quietly, unable yet to understand what had been happening at home. That would come tonight.

Lyan was startled at break when Effie Green came into the yard, looking for him.

'Cass is fine. He hasn't come round from the anaesthetic yet, but Mac says that cut will heal well and he won't even be lame. I wanted to thank you . . .' She looked up at him. 'I don't know what I'd have done if he'd died. He's all I have.'

'Will found him,' Lyan said.

'You brought him to Mac. And you took the children . . . Alison's better without him, but it will still hit her hard,' she said. She wanted to say more, to apologise for her thoughtlessness, to say his scar wasn't as bad as he thought, to try to explain how much Cass meant to her.

She had spent much of the night hunting through the

village gardens, but had not thought to go as far as the farm, not realising that Cass enjoyed the good hunting round the barns, and the company of other cats. By morning she had given up hope, sure that he had been run over and his body disposed of by his killer.

On a sudden impulse, she reached up and kissed Lyan on the cheek. Startled, he took her hands, realising how important the cat was in her life.

'I'm glad he's going to be all right,' he said.

Effie went off to stock up on sardines, which Cass adored. She could fetch him after lunch, Mac had said. She was impatient for the time to pass.

Lyan wondered what he ought to do at the end of the day. Perhaps accompany the children home and make sure that Alison could manage. He was relieved to see Will in the old Land-Rover waiting at the gate.

'Mum sent you this as a thank-you,' he said, flushing as he handed a carrier-bag to the schoolmaster. 'Don't know how we'd have coped without you. It's all tidied up now. My aunt's coming for the night, and the younger children can go home with her for the next few days. Won't matter if they're off school?'

Lyan shook his head. They would all have the weekend in which to recover, as today was Friday. He was thankful he would be able to enjoy the peace of the woods unhindered for the next two days.

Will obviously felt awkward, perhaps thinking of the confidences they had exchanged in the cow byre. The children, racing out, climbed in, even Lucy anxious to find out what had been happening and to see how her mother fared. Will waved as he reversed into the school gateway and turned towards the farm.

Lyan found on investigation that the bag contained a dressed chicken and a dozen eggs.

'Are you going home before the parents arrive?' Miss Carton asked him.

He stared at her in dismay.

'Lord. I'd forgotten.'

'Thought you had.' She was within two years of retiring and hoped he'd take her place. 'Come and eat with me. You aren't expected, are you?'

'Mrs Burton cooks for both of us. I'd better ring. She's not an easy woman at the best of times and the Colonel can suffer if she's annoyed. She would be if I just didn't turn up for a meal she'd cooked.'

It was the first time he had visited the Head's home. Within the past two years they had developed an easy companionship during the day, but had never carried it on beyond working hours. She lived in the next street to the school in a thatched cottage that was one of the features of the village, and was photographed and painted on numerous occasions.

The little sitting-room was warmly welcoming, a log-type gas fire lighting to an instant blaze.

'Nothing like the real thing, but it's fast and labour-saving,' Miss Carton said, laughing as an immense tabby and white cat leaped to her shoulder and sat there, purring at the top of a very considerable voice.

'Suza is far too heavy for such behaviour, but she's done it since she was a kitten,' she said.

'She's huge. Is she a pedigree?'

'She's a Maine Coon. They originated in North America. I'm planning for my retirement. I intend to breed and maybe show.'

Lyan looked at the broad head with its tiger stripes and amazing green eyes. Suza considered him for a moment and then jumped down and wove round his legs.

'She likes you. She isn't very gregarious. She's doing better than I am. You're a very hard man to know, Lyan Grant.'

'Nothing to know.'

'My guess is there's a great deal.' She was already busy

161

in the kitchen. 'I'm feeding us tea and sandwiches. It wouldn't do to greet the parents smelling of whisky, though I suspect that's what you feel like. It's been a trying day.'

'How will the Cartwrights manage?'

'Once the trauma is over, better than they have for years. I used to teach Alison. Marriage addled her wits. She was a competent, sensible girl till she met Jim. He took away all her confidence. Hopefully the farm isn't too much in debt. It would be a tragedy if she lost it.'

'Lucy? How's she going to turn out?'

The room was relaxing him. Comfortable chairs, soft colours, and an amazing array of model elephants in a display cabinet were the only furnishings. The cat, enchanted by this newcomer, had stretched her weighty body on his knees. The little kitchen, through an archway, was almost part of the room.

The sandwiches, of smoked salmon and cucumber, were an unexpected luxury. The coffee was hot, strong and better than any he had tasted.

'I have no relatives left,' Eileen Carton said, stretching herself in the chair on the other side of the fire. 'I indulge myself in small extravagances. Life needs some pleasures.'

She helped herself to two sandwiches. He looked at her with sudden affection. A slender, white-haired woman with amazing dark eyes set deep into her face, she had been an anchor for him, undemanding, supportive, and never intrusive.

'Lucy?' he asked again.

'Lucy worries me. She's her father's daughter and Jim was a pain to teach. If he got an idea into his head he was like a dog with a bone and never let go, even when proved wrong.' The cat had jumped from Lyan's lap and was sitting in front of her owner, her eyes pleading.

Eileen patted her knee, waiting for the invitation to be accepted. Suza stretched, jumped up, tapped her owner's cheek delicately and then circled twice before settling and emitting her deep, throbbing purr.

'If only people were as uncomplicated as animals. Do you realise I've been teaching here for nearly thirty-five years, and have had all the villagers up to the age of forty through the school.'

'There aren't many who can boast of such continuity,' Lyan said. The flickering flames brightened the room, and he focused his eyes on them. The evening was chilly in spite of the time of year. 'Have you never wanted to do anything else? Kick up your heels? Get away from the children?'

'Oddly, no.' She looked at him, contemplating the long, lean body, the scarred side of his face almost hidden against the cushion of the chair, although the position must have been uncomfortable. 'There are days, of course, when I feel I can't stand any more, but mostly I love it. The children come in, and most of them learn. Their achievements are my achievements so that I feel as excited as the tiniest child who has just learnt to read three-word sentences. The first step on the ladder of life.'

Lyan stared into the flames as if they might answer a riddle for him. Eileen ventured a question that had long been in her mind.

'Why did you leave the police? No job satisfaction?'

'I lost my bottle,' Lyan said, feeling the old anger with himself rising. 'I'd have been a danger to others if I'd stayed on. I couldn't do the job any more.'

'That I don't believe. You needed time to come to terms. Anyone would.'

He had never before confided in anyone, keeping his shames and his miseries to himself. Not even the Colonel knew the truth. He was unaware that one of Eileen Carton's great assets was the confidence she inspired in the children, so that they told her secrets they would never have told even to their parents.

163

'Too much happened at once,' he said, gazing back into the past, facing it for the first time. 'My marriage was under strain, as my wife hated the hours I kept, and was having an affair with the man she married after the divorce. That week there had been a particularly nasty murder; I found him. He was the same age as my son; the same height and colouring, and at first I thought it was my own child.'

A car drove down the street outside, and a dog barked from a nearby house. Lyan glanced at the clock. They had an hour before they need go back to the school as everything had been prepared before they left.

'Then came the bank robbery and I was shot. I was in hospital for weeks as they had to rebuild my face, and then they sent me home to convalesce. I got depressed and almost suicidal. My wife couldn't understand and was always angry with me, forcing me to do things, mocking me for my lack of energy and commitment . . .' Only half a man, she'd said, so often he began to believe it. 'I went back again for further operations. Nothing to do but brood.'

Suddenly it was a relief to talk, to share his feelings with someone he knew instinctively was both sympathetic and a safe confidante. He took the scone he was offered without noticing that he was doing so.

'In the end they put me in hospital. The loony bin, my wife called it.' Even now he hated to say her name, 'She visited me twice, and then wrote to say she was leaving and wanted a divorce. She didn't want the children to have anything to do with me.'

'How long were you there?'

'Four months. It was then that Paul came to see me; we'd been at school together and he teaches English at an adult education centre. I think it's a creative writing group and he has a poetry workshop. At first he sat, and then he'd bring poetry books with him and read aloud.

He'd discuss the poems as if I were a pupil—the content, the meaning, the rhythms—and leave the books behind for me to read after he'd gone.'

Suza's purr had risen to a crescendo. Eyes closed, expression blissful, she slowly flexed her claws in and out of her mistress's skirt. Eileen put her hand over the busy paws, and the cat relaxed, sheathing them again.

'Your friend taught you well,' she said. 'The children are beginning to love poetry too.'

'You can find whatever you need,' Lyan said. 'A challenge to change a mood, or words that fit in with it and show you what you're feeling. Paul would pick something with a thumping rhythm if he thought I was particularly down . . .'

"We sleep by the ropes of the camp
And we rise with a shout and we tramp . . ."''

Eileen smiled in sudden delighted recollection.

'I was a bit of a rebel at school,' she said. 'I don't suppose you'd believe it. We had a very solemn English teacher and I liked to shock her. One afternoon we all had to read a poem. I chose the one about the king of Dyfed . . . "His head was borne before us. / His wine and beasts became our feast, / His overthrow our chorus."''

Lyan laughed.

'Our children tend to choose safe subjects, though little Mark Luton surprised me with a poem by Robert Frost about a Morgan colt.'

'Mark has potential. I'll be interested to see how he develops, though I'll be retired long before he's left senior school. Will you stay here?'

'I've no other plans. Except . . .'

'Except what?' she asked as he stopped, confused. Although the Colonel knew of the filming and saw the video after a night on the hill, Lyan had never confessed his real ambition.

'I've been filming the wildlife on Staghill. What I'd really like to do one day is make documentaries, though maybe I can combine that with teaching.'

'I combine my own hobby. I'll do it full time when I retire. I couldn't sit idle.'

She lifted out a folder of prints; hunting scenes, sea scenes, battle scenes, all black and white, and then picked up one that was lying on a small table by the window, a brilliant kaleidoscope.

'They all have to be painted. I find it fascinating. I wanted to be an artist but I was never really good enough to make a living from that.' She picked up a battle scene, horses racing towards the massed enemy, banners flying, a riot of colour. 'I had Mark here recently while I was doing this. His mother had to go to a funeral and had no one else to mind him. I asked him how much more I had to do, thinking he'd say seventeen horses.'

'What did he say?'

'After a long pause, sixty-eight legs!'

Lyan laughed.

'Time we girded our own loins for the fray.' She put the cat on the floor, provoking a squeal of indignation. Suza hated being deprived of her comfort.

'What do I tell Lucy's mother, for goodness sake? I don't know why that child bothers to come to school. She neither listens nor learns.'

Following Eileen across the road, he realised that for most of that visit he had completely forgotten his scar. He felt exhilarated, longing to be free and out on the hill again, listening to the wind in the trees and the soft sound of the rushing water in the far distance.

He no longer dreaded meeting the parents. He could cope again. The past was gone. He could shape his own future. He had a vision of Torran running down the hill with Silver and Missie behind her, and Amber, now forgetting her mistrust of people, trotting alongside, ever protective.

Eileen Carton walked into the big hall that doubled as a gymnasium, and switched on the lights, disclosing ranked chairs and two big tables at which she and Lyan would sit.

'It's always revealing to see who comes and who doesn't,' she said. 'I don't think Lucy's mother will come tonight. Too much to plan and she'll be shattered.'

She walked over to Lyan and touched the scar on his face with gentle fingers.

'It's not nearly as bad as you think. I ceased to notice it months ago ... you draw attention to it. Forget it. I value you as a colleague and tonight I've discovered that there is much more of you than you ever let anyone see.'

He stared at her, startled.

'I'm offering you friendship ... I'd hate to lose touch when I retire. I enjoy our conversations. I hope I haven't offended you?'

Acting on a sudden impulse Lyan bent down and kissed her cheek.

'You've released me from the past,' he said. 'Thank you.'

He turned with a welcoming smile as she opened the door to let in the waiting parents.

Fifteen

There were only two parents outside. The villagers of Lyn-som Green, Lyan always thought, had very little sense of time. The children were often late in the morning; appointments were kept, but it was necessary to allow at least twenty minutes extra before the expected person came. He sat watching Eileen Carton exert her consider-able charm and waited hopefully for more to arrive.

They had spent a great deal of energy on the room during the week, cleaning, tidying, and adorning the walls with the children's drawings. Mark Luton had produced a very lifelike horse rearing, mane flying, tail in the air, forehooves flailing in front of him. He had great hopes for young Mark.

He had hesitated before putting up Lucy Cartwright's masterpiece. It was undoubtedly well executed and con-siderably better than the efforts of most of her classmates. For all that it worried him. The figure tied to a tree, surrounded by flames, was obviously female. Behind her, almost hidden in smoke, were two deer, one of them white.

'She's been reading about our local witch,' Eileen Carton said. 'If you remember, the legend has it that she always went about with a white stag. I'm sure it's not meant to represent Torran.'

Lyan was uneasy as he looked at it again. Lucy had painted it that afternoon. He remembered her saying 'I like fire', when she wrote her verse, and she had been more animated than he had ever seen her that day, talking about words that described it.

He straightened the exercise books laid out on the tables for the parents to see. He wished he were up on the hill, out in the woods, watching the small movements of the night. Owl and badger, fox and cat, they all had an innocence that was lacking in humans.

The woman who came into the room at that moment was a stranger to him. She nodded uneasily, glanced at Eileen Carton, still busy with her own visitors, and walked over to the table nearest to Lyan, searching among the books until she found what she wanted.

She was a small woman, delicately made, wearing white jeans and a patterned floral anorak that must have come from abroad. Her tawny hair curled round a delicately boned face. As she turned to him, enormous dark eyes filled, to his astonishment, with pain, he recognised her. She could only be Mark's mother. No one could mistake those eyes. They watched him throughout the day.

'It's not fair,' she said, unexpectedly. Lyan raised one eyebrow, taking care to turn the unscarred side of his face towards her. He was healing, but sensitivity was not overcome in a moment.

'What's not fair?'

'This.'

She held out the book with Mark's poem on loneliness. 'It's just not true. At least, not in the way he means.'

Tears overflowed, and Lyan, embarrassed, went to the refreshment table and poured a cup of coffee for her, bringing one for himself as well. Eileen prided herself on her coffee and her cakes. He wondered what they would do when she retired.

'I'm sorry. It's just ... why is life so difficult?' Celia Luton demanded, overpowering him again with the full impact of her astonishing eyes.

'Tell me.' As yet there were very few people there, and there was plenty of time.

She drank her coffee, and then unzipped the jacket,

revealing a white sweater embroidered with flowers. The tiny gold horse brooch at her throat was obviously the model for Mark's drawing.

'My husband was made redundant three years ago. He was manager of one of the small factories on the industrial estate in Pyneton. The receivers came in, and they were sold to another firm who stripped the assets and closed them down.'

It was a familiar story and one that always infuriated Lyan.

'John was out of work for six months. It was a bad time and we all suffered, especially Mark, who is far too sensitive. I seemed to be a permanent buffer between them, as Mark was too young to understand what was happening to his father, and managed to irritate him constantly.'

The room was beginning to fill up, but most of the parents headed for the refreshments table, to help themselves to coffee or tea and the cakes and sausage rolls. Lyan, glancing across at the spread, realised Eileen must have worked for hours. She saw his gaze and smiled at him, so that he surprised himself by a sudden feeling of affection. She had eased his path for him during the past years.

He rallied his thoughts. Celia Luton was still speaking, overcome by a need to unburden herself.

'John has found a job, but it's with an oil company and we never know where he will be sent next; it may be Aberdeen, or out in the Middle East. It may be for a month, or six months. This time he's in Saudi Arabia for a year. We hate it, but he's no choice; he's tried for other jobs. We need the money. He's a trained engineer. The pay's far better than he had before. He's away now for such long stretches at a time.' Her voice broke suddenly and she paused for a moment to recover. 'I think Mark's sure we're on the point of splitting up, and he worries about it. I tell him it's nonsense which is the truth, but you know what children are when they get an idea into their heads.'

Lyan took the coffee cups to refill and brought back plates for each of them—almond buns, sausage rolls, and two pieces of Dundee cake which took him back to his own childhood and his mother offering it as 'cut and come again' cake.

'To make matters worse,' Celia Luton said, lifting a sausage roll and looking at it as if she had never seen such a thing before, 'my horses have recently begun to win at the shows and there's a demand for foals. I feel I must go on, as one can't rely on any job lasting these days and they bring in good money. I school them for dressage and am beginning to be asked for displays. I do spend all the time I can spare with Mark, but there are long hours when he has to be alone . . . I listen to him, but he doesn't say very much at all.'

Lyan had a vision of the silent house, of the child absorbed in his own affairs, and the woman who needed occupation to fill the lonely months until her husband came home again. Maybe there was a solution to one part of her problems.

'Mark's nearly eleven,' he said. 'He's a mature little boy for his age, and growing up fast. Can't you involve him with the horses? Give him a foal of his own to care for, and maybe share in the money you get for it, even if it's only a fraction of the price you receive. Involve him in the family affairs.'

'He hates the horses.'

'I don't think so. He read us a Robert Frost poem, about a little Morgan, left out in the cold and snow, and terrified. You should have heard the passion in his voice. He was really angry even to think that anyone could treat a horse so. He had a quarrel with Lucy Cartwright who was scathing about the fuss over an animal born to live outdoors.'

She looked down at the exercise book she was still holding.

'I read him the poem one night. I had no idea it made any impression. He's very uncommunicative. He just looks at you and you don't know what he's thinking. Did he really sound as if he cared?'

'Believe me, he did. Try, anyway. It may not be easy . . . he isn't an easy child, I know.' He thought of the many times he had tried to draw Mark out of his shell, of the uncompromising brown-eyed stare, the unreadable expression. He was a child who walked alone and, apart from Shelley, seemed not to take any notice of the other children, avoiding them whenever possible.

Celia read out the last two lines of her son's poem:

'I wish I had a cat.
I could cuddle that.'

'I can get him a kitten. I never thought of it. He never asked for one.' She smiled at Lyan, her face suddenly illuminated. 'Thank you. You've helped me a lot. I do get depressed when John's away for so long. You can't really talk in the same way to a child as to an adult, and I can't share my worries with him, or even with John now. It would upset him if he thought I was suffering. He's keeping us and paying the mortgage . . . all the wretched commitments one has in society today. I often envy the Ardans. They seem to lead such a simple life.'

Lyan thought of them surviving as best they could, trying to live down memories that still obsessed both of them. He wondered how the cat and the cub were faring and whether they were still alive. He would call in on his way home.

'The house, Mark, and the horses take all my time. You can't socialise with animals to care for. And the village doesn't take outsiders to its heart, as I expect you know.'

Lyan watched her walk across the room and continue to look at Mark's books, a smile on her lips. He had completely forgotten about his scarred face, and was startled when another woman, whom he had never seen before, came across to him, saw the puckering and hastily turned away, as if caught spying. Eileen Carton, looking across the room, saw the reaction and put her thumb up to encourage him.

By the end of the evening he was exhausted. He was tired of using tact, of reassuring couples who were certain their offspring had no aptitude at all, and others who were full of their child's achievements and overestimated his or her ability. The Browns, with their expectations for their son of an Oxford scholarship that was far beyond his capabilities, were dismayed when he suggested that the boy should be encouraged in his woodwork, as he excelled at that.

He sighed as he watched them leave. The father, a bank manager, had no time at all for those who did not gain academic achievements. Their child, struggling to understand anything but the simplest concepts, was probably doomed to a very unhappy adolescence. All his skill was in his fingers. They had dismissed the enchanting little clipper that he had made in woodwork, which was proudly displayed on a stand of its own.

Among those who tried his patience was Councillor Prentice, who eulogised on his son, and his cleverness. The boy was as devious as his father, Lyan thought. Before he quite realised what was happening, the man launched into a political diatribe detailing what in his view, the country needed most—more urbanisation, more roads, more towns, and far less of a countryside no longer required as all farmers overproduced and nobody wanted their products any more.

The headache that had been threatening all day suddenly intensified so that Lyan found it hard to concentrate. He was thankful when at last the Councillor decided it was time he went home.

Celia Luton was still looking at her son's exercise books.

'Effie Green's with Mark tonight,' she said, catching the schoolmaster's glance. 'I wanted to have a good look at his work so that I could talk about it when I came home.'

'Effie?'

'I know she's a wicked old gossip, but, oddly, she can be very kind. She looked after Mark when I had flu and got Will Cartwright to come and see to the horses. You've made an impression on her. She's telling everyone how you rescued her cat and took him to the vet, and how he owes his life to you.'

'Will rescued the cat.'

'You carried him down the hill, and that she felt, was a labour of love as he's heavy and was distressed, and you were covered in his blood. All over your jacket and you didn't even care.' She sat down on the chair again. 'You look exhausted. George Prentice is enough to wear anyone out.'

Lyan sighed.

'His son is as wearing as he is.'

It was a relief when the room was empty and the last footsteps had died away.

'We've finished early tonight, thank heaven,' Eileen Carton said. 'I'm bushed. How do you feel about leaving all this and coming in tomorrow to get it cleared up so that it's clear for Monday? I know it's Saturday, but we can't really leave it till Monday. Would you like to come home for that drink?'

Lyan sighed at the thought of his interrupted weekend, but there was no choice.

'Tomorrow morning's fine. If I come in and sit down I'll never get up again,' he said, yawning. 'I'll get back to the Place.'

'There's enough coffee left for the two of us and I'm

sure you can manage the last two sausage rolls; they're horrible when they're stale.' She poured out two more cups, balancing herself on the edge of the table. 'Effie Green said she'd come in first thing and wash up for us. She's a wicked old woman and sometimes I suspect her of deliberate mischief-making, but she has a good heart.'

She laughed at his expression.

'She'd be the last to admit that. She looks after children when parents have emergencies; she visits whenever anyone she knows is ill in hospital; she made a lot of the cakes tonight.'

'She looked after Mark Luton when his mother had flu,' Lyan said.

'There you are, then.'

*   *   *

A Hunter's Moon, he thought, as he turned out of the village street on to the track to his home. He never used his little runabout on his daily trip to school, feeling the mile walk did him more good.

Tonight he looked forward to the quiet beneath the trees and the solitude. He was in no hurry and strolled slowly, aware of a softly hooting owl and the faraway answer, of a rustle in the bushes that might be mouse or bird. There had been a gale forecast and the wind was rising, bending the trees, moaning among the branches.

Dead leaves blew along the ground. There was an eerie wailing in the air, as if the whole world was throbbing with hidden forces. The noise surrounded him. It would be a wild night. Stars glittered in a clear sky.

For all that, the familiar peace began to exert its healing influence. A thumping in the distance told of the old boar badger, sitting and scratching vigorously, just as the dogs did. He would take them out for a last walk before turning in. He knew the Colonel's arthritic hip was paining him and that they would only have romped in the garden.

175

Neither man went to bed before midnight and it was not yet ten.

He was irritated when he saw a figure coming down the path. He recognised Dorothy Burton and, aware that he was hidden by the trees, he slipped off the track and flattened himself against a trunk. He had no desire for conversation. He wondered why she was there. Perhaps to post a letter as she would be busy in the morning. His guess was confirmed when he saw the white envelope in her hand.

He was startled when she stopped at the two mailboxes, opened that belonging to the Ardans, and put the letter inside. A white envelope! He waited until she had gone and then took it out, recognising the black print. So she was the anonymous letter-writer. He tore it open, his worst fears confirmed.

Infuriated, he ran, catching her easily before she reached the branch of the track that led to the Place.

'Mrs Burton.'

She turned and saw the envelope and letter in his hand. It was too dark to see the small print but the three lines spoke for themselves and the word BEWARE was printed in such huge capitals that he could read it by moonlight.

She looked at the page and then at him, and set her lips, saying nothing.

'Why?' he asked. 'What harm have they ever done you?'

'Harm? What harm?' She was suddenly unable to contain her fury. 'All of you, battening on his good nature, taking everything he has to give, contributing nothing. What does he get for harbouring you all? Too good to live, the Colonel is, and never knowing how you take advantage.'

'What on earth are you talking about?' Lyan felt he had wandered into realms of insanity.

'How many others live rent free, conning him, that we

don't know about? And her, she's no better than she ought to be, even the Colonel out night after night with her at first till you came and took her from him. Think I don't know where you spend your nights? And the man she lives with . . . he's no more her grandfather than I am . . . the villagers hate them, and rightly, too.'

Her voice was rising and Lyan could only stare at her, appalled. How had they never guessed at the venom that lay behind that quiet demeanour?

'The cottage should be mine; my own home, not two rooms in someone else's house. If they weren't there the Colonel would've let me live there.'

'He tells me it was a ruin when you came. The Ardans worked on it. They paid for the materials and did most of the repairing themselves to make it habitable and I assure you they pay rent and so do I.'

'I never expected two men and two dogs to look after when I came here. There was just him and me, and we got on fine. I'm not a young woman . . .'

He didn't want to consider the thought that came into his head but he was too angry to refrain from saying it.

'Did you poison Sapphire?'

She glared up at him, her small grey eyes glittering with hate.

'I did. And I wish she'd died. Quint never did take food from me and then you taught them both to refuse it from anyone but the two of you. He kept them out of my kitchen and away from me; always sleeping in his room, a dirty habit. I never got another chance. If I had they wouldn't be here, either of them. Horrible beasts.'

Had the Colonel suspected? Lyan wondered. And would she poison me, if she'd poison them? It was not a pleasant thought, and he pushed it away guiltily.

'The Ardans'll not be here much longer, I promise you that.' There was triumph in the woman's voice. Lyan, shocked by her revelations, had a sudden desire to catch

177

her by the throat and shake the life from her. Trembling with rage, he thrust his hands into his pockets.

He was about to ask her what she meant when he heard a sudden outcry from above. A small herd of deer bounded down the ride, leaping aside when they saw the two human figures. Behind them raced Silver with Missie beside him and Amber at his heels.

The wailing continued, a noisy sobbing, accompanied by thudding feet as Lucy Cartwright, crying at the top of her voice, rushed down the track.

Lyan put out a hand but she dodged him and ran on, still crying. Her face was suffused, her eyes screwed up, and she radiated terror. He turned to look after her, and caught a glimpse out of the corner of his eye that sickened him.

Flames were leaping into the sky. The cottage was on fire. Black smoke poured towards him, dark on the rising wind, above it leaping tongues of yellow and scarlet. He forgot Dorothy Burton as he raced up the track that led off to the Ardans' home, slowing to catch his breath as a stitch knifed through his side.

A moment later he realised that it was not the cottage that was on fire but the shelter in which the deer had slept with the spaniel. That, the walls creosoted, the roof tarred, was well alight. Wind fanned the flames and he watched in horror as they blew across the gap and through the open kitchen window, the curtains at once flaring. The air was rank. He found it hard to breathe as smoke swirled about him.

He thundered on the door.

Sixteen

Lucy bolted, overcome by terror. She wanted Will, who represented sanity. Her mother was always racing from one job to another, too busy to listen to her.

She had been afraid of her father, of his strange moods, of his frequent rages, of his impatience, which had been getting worse in the past few months. Home was a place to avoid, and she had found refuge with Davey up on the hill.

The children had made a den among the bushes, roofed over with branches, in the best story-book style. Here they could meet. They were both lonely, for Davey had no brothers and sisters, and there was a big gap between Will and Lucy, and three years between her and the next in the family. They told each other stories, both intending to be writers when they grew up, which made a bond between them.

Dorothy Burton had met them by accident a year before. Davey had fallen and cut his knee, and she took him into the Place and bathed and bandaged the injury. She gave the children hot cocoa and buttered scones. She enjoyed talking to them as they were uncritical and listened avidly to her stories.

Davey's mother sent her a small box of chocolates as a thank-you for her kindness to her son. The children began to call often, always ready for a drink and cakes, being far less critical than the Colonel of her baking, and there was always home-made fudge which they both adored. She kept it in a large square tin with a picture of the Houses of Parliament on the lid.

They could do things that she could not, and, what was more, she'd never be suspected. Lucy took some of the letters to put in the mailbox, though she had no idea of the contents. Davey kept the housekeeper informed of all that was happening, of schemes that his father had let slip, unaware that his son was listening.

She enjoyed the feeling of power, of knowing things that neither the Colonel nor the schoolmaster knew, which might affect their future. She told the children stories, which she read up in the library, about the old cottage and Mad Mag.

They had put her in the lake to see if she would drown or float. If she drowned she was innocent. Her survival of the ordeal by water proved her wickedness, and the witch-hunters condemned her to death by burning.

Mad Mag had been the village midwife, but many of the babies and some of the mothers had died. She cast her spells on cattle and sheep, on farm and cottage, on child and adult, and she brought sickness and death. That might all have happened in the eighteenth century, but her descendants lived and thrived and wickedness flourished. Evil is with us all the time, the housekeeper said, discovering an unexpected flair for both acting and story-telling.

Davey and Lucy were entranced. Dorothy Burton brought home books on the old witches from the library and mixed small facts with large fictions, jealousy feeding her tongue.

She told her enthralled audience how wicked the foreign woman was, how she sacrificed animals and buried them in the garden. They had graves like household pets, but that was a cover-up. She couldn't fool Dorothy Burton, who knew how to recognise evil.

The small graves were easy to see from the path that ran behind the cottage garden. Davey and Lucy looked at them with a feeling of terror that was almost pleasurable.

Maybe Torran was like the witch in 'Hansel and Gretel' and would capture them and feed them up and then eat them. They always ran past the cottage.

Dorothy's hatred grew. Torran seemed to have everything that she had never had. She was attractive, she was young, she was admired by the three men, who were, the housekeeper was sure, her secret lovers. This story, she knew, was also current in the village. Still waters run deep, the landlady of the Dog and Duck said. No smoke without fire, said Tom McToul.

Above all, the Ardans had the cottage which, Dorothy Burton had convinced herself, should have been hers and would have been if they had never come. She had coveted it from the moment she saw it, and dreamed constantly of making it her own.

The fact that Torran was a witch was a secret, she told the children, just between the three of them, and they mustn't talk about it at all. Lucy, unable to keep total silence, told Will, who laughed at her, but since her father also swore that Torran had bewitched his cattle, she knew Will was wrong.

She hadn't told him the source of her story. Mrs Burton assured them she knew ways of protecting them from the witch, but she said that the protection wouldn't last if they told anyone at all about her.

Lucy, who spent much of her spare time watching television, half-believing the stories and sure that all the characters in the various series were real people, found it easy to believe that one of her neighbours was a witch. She found an old horseshoe and kept it beside her bed.

It was the housekeeper who had suggested the children taunt Torran in the wood, and told them what to say. The intervention of the schoolmaster infuriated her. She had been watching, hidden behind the trees.

Davey and Lucy knew better than to try that again, lest it came to his ears. They had, most of the time, a healthy respect for him, and knew that major bouts of naughtiness would not be tolerated.

Lyan had his own punishment for any child who transgressed. He or she was chosen, for a week, or more if the crime warranted it, to spend breaks and lunch hours stocktaking, making correctly spelt and legible lists of the contents of the stationery cupboards. Few wanted to do it a second time, though Lucy had done it three times and Davey four. Lyan suspected their memories were shorter than their capacity for mischief.

Dorothy Burton had hoped that the accumulation of the letters and the children's animosity would drive the Ardans away. Then she could have her own home at last, and still look after the Colonel, who would get rid of the schoolmaster, she was sure, if the Ardans went. She would be able to achieve a longstanding ambition: her own colour schemes and furnishing; her own privacy: a front door to lock out the world and her own space beyond it. In the twenty years since her husband had died, she had had none of these things.

She convinced Lucy that Torran was responsible for sickness in the cattle. Will said it was mastitis due to his father's neglect but Will was wrong. Lucy knew that. He told her not to believe everything she heard, that people made up stories for their own purposes. He thought that probably Effie was responsible for this one and dismissed it as childish nonsense. Lucy was very young for her age in some ways and had too much imagination. He was too busy to spare more than a passing thought for his young sister's beliefs.

Lucy knew that the deer was a ghost creature, a familiar, like the cats of the old witches. This witch was too clever to have a cat: people might then recognise her for what she was. Only Mrs Burton knew the truth. Nobody could hide their true nature from her. She gave the children the impression of having immense knowledge.

Instead of a cat, Dorothy told them, the witch had conjured up a devil from the past and given him the shape of a white deer. The old-time witch had also had a white deer, a ghost deer. He vanished the day she died. That was pure invention but it could have happened, and would have happened, she persuaded herself.

Lucy was sure that the witch had caused her father's death. No doubt about that. If she were not stopped, there would be other deaths in the family; all of them in the end. A calf had died two weeks ago, born the wrong way round. The vet hadn't reached them in time. That was the witch again: her mark would be on all the herd. Soon they would have no cows at all, and no income, and how would they live then?

The children listened avidly, frightened but intrigued. Davey, a little older than Lucy and more cautious, became alarmed at the talk of driving the witch away, and freeing the village of her influence. The children could set the little shed on fire; that would make the witch and the man she called her grandfather afraid, and they would leave. The cottage would not be harmed as the shed was away from it. The cottage must remain intact.

Dorothy Burton provided the matches. Davey, shocked into sense, failed to convince Lucy that this was a pretty rotten idea. He made off home, wanting nothing to do with it, but was too frightened to tell either of his parents. Lucy was to toss the matches into the straw. No one would ever know what had caused the fire—maybe some tramp hiding and smoking. No one would ever suspect Lucy.

If the witch went, everything would be all right again, Lucy told herself. The thought of starting a blaze excited her. Fire flash and flame and flicker. There would be engines and people there fast to put it out, the housekeeper told her. No real harm would be done. It would convince Torran and Jan that they would be better away from Lynsom Green. The barn fire had been exciting too.

Nobody knew how that had started. Neither Lucy nor Davey ever confessed to smoking in the hay.

The events of the past day had deprived Lucy of her small amount of common sense. Her mother was distracted. Will was so busy with the animals that he had no time for her, and she had little to do with the younger children, who played together, excluding her. Dorothy Burton listened to her, and she trusted her. The witch had caused her father's death. Will was stupid.

Nobody liked her and nobody wanted her. They'd all thank her in time because she had driven the witch away. One day she'd tell them. She had finally been convinced of Torran's wickedness when she told Dorothy Burton that her father had lost his spaniel. Jim Cartwright had not told his family of the sale, wanting the money for himself. All they knew was that the dog had vanished and good riddance to her as she'd been nothing but a pest.

Lucy had loved the spaniel. The little animal was lonely and so was the child, who often crept into the barn and cuddled down in the straw, holding the small body tightly, savouring the licking tongue. Dorothy Burton seized on the information and told the children that the spaniel had last been seen at the cottage and was undoubtedly now lying in one of the small graves. Amber, trusting no one but Torran and Jan, was never seen outside the cottage; she hid from all passers-by.

Lucy, afraid now, gave the cottage a wide berth so that the dog did not scent her. Had she done so, she would have run to greet her. Such wickedness, Dorothy Burton said, and the children believed her.

The shed would burn but not the cottage. Lucy repeated that over and over as a talisman. The witch wouldn't be hurt but the fire would alarm her, and she would leave. Maybe it wouldn't bring her father back to life again, but Lucy wasn't even sure she wanted that. It had always been more peaceful when he was away from home.

It was only when the straw began to burn that Lucy saw the animals, who had been curled together at the back of the shed. The door was never shut, so that they could wander as they chose and often slipped out at night to explore their surroundings. Hearing her footsteps they had kept very still, hoping to avoid human eyes.

Lucy lit one match and threw it into the darkness, tossing in the open matchbox so that there was a sudden whoosh of light. As the fire flashed into life the animals fled, Silver knocking Lucy over. A very real stag indeed, and behind him came the little one, and after her the spaniel, all so terrified by the flames that they sped into the darkness.

The deer was a real deer; the dog wasn't dead, but looking bonnier than she ever had when she lived with them. The leaping fire had taken possession, was devouring the straw, was teasing at the wooden walls which flashed into a roaring furnace. There was another shed beyond it and the wind was tossing the burning sparks.

A spark landed on Lucy's wrist and she ran, choking back the screams. She didn't know what to do. The wind had taken charge so that within minutes there was a raging inferno, the creosoted wood and tarred roof providing ready fuel. Lucy felt sick with fright.

She ought to hammer on the cottage door and warn them, but what did they do to people who set places on fire? She might go to prison . . . awful things happened to you if the police found out. Nobody must find out.

Nobody would believe her if she said that Mrs Burton had told her to set fire to the shed and drive away the witch. The rising gale was screaming through the trees, was driving sparks into the air. The hill was bright with an uncanny glow and wild with noise.

Suppose the woods caught? Suppose the flames leaped

to the cottage? Suppose the witch and her grandfather were burned to death? Suppose the wind spread the fire to the trees, to their own farmhouse, the flames springing like live beasts from one place to another? The barns would catch, and the animals would be burned . . .

She had seen mountain fires on television, but had not thought that this could get so out of hand so fast. Only the shed, Mrs Burton had said. It won't spread. But they hadn't thought of the wind . . .

Would they accuse her of murder?

The deer wasn't a ghost. He had knocked her over and hurt her, his body only too solid. The spaniel wasn't dead . . . what else was untrue? The thoughts went round in her head, tormenting her until her flying feet took her back to the farm, to her only safety, her terrified wails echoing among the trees as she ran.

Behind her, the animals were already galloping for shelter. Away from the smell of burning that tainted the air. Away from the crackle and hiss and the black smoke that choked them. Away from the red glare that terrified them. Away from the thumping feet of the racing child. Away from a danger that they had never met before but which they knew threatened them all.

Will, exhaustedly cleaning up the dairy after making a meal for the family, heard Lucy's bawling and thought, 'Oh God! What now?'

His mother, convinced that her own neglect had killed her husband, was in bed, heavily sedated. At eighteen, he had all the responsibility and he couldn't take any more.

Seventeen

The cottage was unusually quiet. Mac had called that morning to look at the cat and the cub: both were in shock, lying unnaturally still, fear of their strange surroundings adding to the trauma. The bites were deep, and showing signs of infection in spite of the injections.

'It happens,' he said, sighing. 'We need something stronger. Modern medicine is marvellous, but there's always a chance that the first drug we try won't work.'

He had taken them both to his little hospital, to put them on a drip, promising to let Torran know as soon as there was any improvement. She refused to contemplate anything else.

She was painting, totally engrossed, portraying the woods as they had been the year before—four cubs playing in a tiny glade, their mother watching over them. Jan frowned thoughtfully as he completed the carving of his charging bull.

The sudden pounding on the door startled them. Torran's brush flew across the canvas. Jan jumped and the knife he was using bit into the gap between his thumb and first finger. Cursing, he padded it with tissues. Torran stared at him. Both of them were pitchforked back into Africa, when the night had gone wild.

'Torran, Jan . . .' Lyan was yelling, suddenly afraid they might have been in the shed with the animals. Jan recognised his voice and ran. The door to the kitchen was shut and he had no idea that the house was on fire.

'For God's sake, man . . .'

'The shed's on fire . . . So is your kitchen . . .'

'Amber . . . the deer . . .' Torran flew past him to rescue her charges. Jan was already by the telephone, dialling. Lyan raced after Torran. He grabbed her arm.

'They're safe. I saw them running away, all three of them. Where's your hose?'

'Hanging inside the shed.' Torran looked at him helplessly. The wooden walls were burning fiercely, and she had been unable to get near. There was no chance of rescuing that. Lyan turned his head as the Colonel's Land-Rover rocketed to a standstill and he leaped out.

'Saw the fire . . .'

'The other shed,' Torran said, and ran, the two men following. The corner of the second building was already alight. She flung open the door. Neither the Colonel nor Lyan had realised just how many birds and small animals she had there in her little hospital.

Jan was back with a bucket of water which he flung, causing a hissing and some slight diminution of the flames, but little change. The fire had already taken hold.

'Form a chain . . .' The Colonel picked up a cage and thrust it at Lyan. He passed it to Torran, and Jan ran with it to the road, well away from the house. This was going to take for ever. They were lost in a scene from hell, every moment precious, as they might not be able to save all the terrified creatures.

Headlights lanced across the sky as a Land-Rover and two cars sped up the track. Will Cartwright jumped out, followed by several of his neighbours. Within minutes the men had formed a line and the cages were being brought out fast. Several had buckets which they filled from the stream, but the water had little effect. More cars appeared and more people joined them, among them a number of women. Lyan recognised familiar faces. The cages passed swiftly from hand to hand.

'That's the lot,' the Colonel said. The heat was intense and he had a burnt hand. A sudden gust of wind fanned the flames, and the second shed collapsed. The fire in the kitchen had spread; the downstairs windows were cracking. The newcomers felt helpless.

The wind had no mercy. As it increased in strength the flames leaped high, smoke billowing to the sky, shadows spreading eerily.

Lyan was reminded of Lucy's poem: 'Flare and flicker, / Flame and flash . . .' Lucy! Had she done this? Sirens sounded on the air, coming nearer at speed. Fire engine, police car. Help had arrived, but too late. They were thankful to let the professionals take charge, to pump water from the stream, so that their hoses dowsed the remains of the sheds and hissed on the cottage, which was now well alight.

Lyan, seeing the figures illuminated in the darkness, wondered if the whole village had come to watch. Will, his face blackened and one hand thrust into his shirt, smarting with the pain of a burn, walked across to Lyan.

'Lucy . . .' he said.

'Did she start it?'

'That housekeeper of the Colonel's . . . always talking to her and Davey. Told them Torran was a witch and witches must burn. Told them she sacrifices small animals and showed them the graves. Told Lucy that she'd put a spell on our farm, and if she didn't put an end to it, then the whole village would suffer. She was so scared it all came pouring out when she came home. Weird. She thought Torran had caused our dad's death . . . she was avenging him. He always had time for Lucy—when he was sober.'

He paused, his expression miserable.

'She only meant to burn the shed and scare them away . . . never thought about the wind . . . She's only a kid . . .'

'That's insane,' Lyan said, appalled. He thought of the letter in his pocket. Surely the woman would never have influenced the child and persuaded her to burn the place

189

down. He had a sudden memory of the strange behaviour of people he had come across in his police career. Some of them had been very hard to understand, and had indulged in appalling wickedness, startling friends and neighbours alike.

'Reckon the damned woman is crazy.' Will stared miserably at the burning cottage. Nobody seemed able to move. They were all watching, oblivious of time. 'Thing is, our Lucy, she loves animals, and the thought of them being killed . . . when she set light to the shed the deer came out, and the spaniel. The big deer knocked her over and she knew then he wasn't a ghost, but real . . . she saw the little one and recognised the dog.'

Will put a hand to his face, which was singed from the flames.

'Dad told us he'd lost it. Just run off. But the house-keeper told her Torran had stolen it to sacrifice, and that it was buried out there, in the garden.'

Lyan wondered if any of them could have convinced Lucy that she was wrong. That essay she had written . . . he had thought it childish silliness and though it worried him he had not realised that she was sincere in her miscon-ceptions.

'When she saw the spaniel she knew it was all lies, that there might be other animals inside and she'd be the one that killed them . . . it was hard to get out of her. She's in a bad way. I had to get the doctor.'

'Dear God,' the Colonel said. Neither Will nor Lyan had noticed him approach and he had heard most of the story. Jan and Torran were standing side by side, looking at the wreckage around them. Torran saw flames in another country and men shouting, and was unable to stop shak-ing. She couldn't believe that she had lost a second home and that the nightmare had returned, to a place she thought of as a sanctuary.

Somebody had brought blankets and put one round

her shoulders, but Jan could feel her shivering as he held his arm around her. He had not yet realised that the fire was deliberate, though he could not imagine how it had started.

High on Staghill the animals congregated, hiding from the madness that had overtaken the night. The hoses were now soaking the undergrowth, making sure that the fire could not spread to the woods. The last flames flickered and died, leaving black ash, soaked and filthy.

'You'll come home with us,' the Colonel said, going over to the Ardans, who stood helplessly watching.

'What about the animals?'

Lyan was examining the cages. A young owl gazed at him out of enormous eyes, as still as if it were stuffed. Four baby hedgehogs huddled together. Many of the other cages contained birds, among them a pheasant with an injured wing. Five tiny blind kittens, cuddled up against one another, mewed softly as it was feeding time.

'Some of the children bring them,' Jan said. 'Young Mark Luton is a genius at finding injured creatures. He leaves them on the doorstep . . . never comes in or speaks to us. Mac brings us his wild patients—the owl was hit by a car and was concussed. The pheasant is another road traffic victim. Usually we can release them.'

He grinned suddenly, a smoke-blackened hobgoblin.

'The trouble is the birds come back, knowing where to find a free hand-out. They cost us a fortune.'

'They can go in the garden room,' the Colonel said, referring to what had once been an immense scullery. Now it housed wellingtons and dog leads, various tools and watering-cans and the washing machine and a large deep freeze.

'It's big enough for all of them, and more too. We've bedrooms to spare.'

Will, desperately anxious to make amends for his sister's guilt, loaded his Land-Rover with the cages. The Ardans, still speechless, climbed into the Colonel's vehicle. Torran clung to Jan's hand, needing reassurance.

'Should be safe now,' one of the firemen said, as Lyan walked across to them. 'We'll stay on, just in case.'

Lyan looked at the smouldering ruins of the sheds, at the wrecked cottage, only two rooms intact, and those would be soaked and blackened. Most of it had gone. He wondered if it could be restored, or would have to be pulled down and a new place put up. Centuries of history had been destroyed in a few hours.

The village women had turned out in force, shocked at the disaster. It needed little imagination to guess how it felt to be suddenly homeless, without any possessions but the clothes they were wearing. Everyone had been too busy saving the birds and animals to salvage anything from the cottage. By the time the last cage was safely away from the fire, it was blazing fiercely and no one could get near.

Effie Green and Mary Dunnet had brought flasks with them and handed out coffee, some of the other women helping. Lyan saw faces that were totally unknown to him.

'Need help up at the house?' Effie asked. 'A lot of people to take care of.' Without asking if she might, she joined him as he made his way up the track.

They arrived to find further chaos. Dorothy Burton, so enraged that she was barely articulate, was shouting at the Colonel, though the words were almost unintelligible. Lyan wondered if she were drunk.

Inside the house Sapphire and Quint were barking furiously, making so much noise that they failed to recognise familiar voices. They were rarely left alone and had no intention of letting anyone in. The housekeeper had been forced to wait outside. With the realisation that the blaze had spread to the cottage, the last strands of her sanity had given way.

She had not intended the cottage to burn, although

192

she wanted to drive the occupants away. She did not know if they were safe. She had not wanted their deaths . . . only to scare them, since they had ignored her threatening letters.

She turned, saw Torran, and gave way to hysteria, yelling at her, blaming her for everything that had happened. Torran, white-faced, was speechless, unable to understand the reason for such fury. Will, who was nearest, grabbed her by the arm and pushed her into the Land-Rover, shutting the door on her, afraid that the housekeeper might harm her.

'You too,' Dorothy Burton shouted at Jan. 'Think I don't know . . . ?'

Melissa walked over to her and took her arm.

'Now, now, my dear,' she said. 'You're upsetting yourself. It won't do. We'll go up to your rooms. I'll make you a nice hot cup of tea and you can have a rest. It's been a trying night.'

Dorothy Burton looked at her blankly. She was confused and exhausted, but followed the vicar's wife and waited beside her, well away from the people who had come to offer help, activated by pity and remorse. None of them had wanted this.

There was silence as the Colonel opened the front door, speaking to the dogs who, recognising him once he was inside with them, greeted him fervently. He shut them in his den, leaving the way free for everyone else. There seemed to be dozens of willing hands helping Will unload the cages.

Lyan took a deep breath of relief when he heard a familiar voice, and went to greet the doctor.

'Anyone hurt tonight? My wife told me when I got home. She can't leave the children, but says if there's anything she can do tomorrow, to let her know. Had a man with a perforated ulcer. Halfway to Pineton. Then young Lucy. Couldn't come before.'

'I think we need you upstairs, doctor,' Effie said. Her hair was untidy, her face grey, showing exhaustion. Lyan realised that she was much older than she pretended. Jason looked at Torran, who was lying back in a chair, her face white, still shivering.

'I'm all right,' she said, though her teeth were chattering. She looked at Lyan. 'Silver . . . Amber . . . Missie . . . You're quite sure they're safe? You weren't just trying to stop me getting burned?'

'They'll be looking for you tomorrow,' Lyan promised, his mind filled with the need for hot drinks, hot-water bottles, and blankets. He glanced at the clock: four a.m. There was not much of the night left.

Torran needed a bed, and Jan was grey-faced and moved as if he had aged twenty years in the last few hours. Both Will and the Colonel needed treatment for burns. His own hands were scorched: he had only just begun to notice the pain. He felt sick with misery. Could this have been prevented? Reason told him that they could not have known what was in Mrs Burton's mind.

'People are unexpected,' Roger said, surprised to find so many volunteers, as Melissa appeared with a tray of mugs and a pot of coffee. Her husband brought a large dish filled with small cakes, sandwiches and pasties. The baker had come with half his stock. Food, the universal panacea, Lyan thought, realising that he was, in fact, extremely hungry.

'I don't know what's going on.' Donald Trent, offering the plate, looked bemused. 'Effie rang . . . said the cottage was on fire. Thought they'd need beds, so Melissa and I came . . . Someone said it was deliberate.'

'Never mind, love. I'll explain later.' Melissa seemed able to carry on all night if necessary. Within an hour she had organised several women who had appeared from nowhere to help make up beds. Effie was asked to stay with Dorothy Burton, who had relapsed into total silence and refused both food and drink. Jason Hall, trying to talk to her, found himself baffled.

Effie, sensing that her presence might be the cause of that particular problem, left the room. Her leaving unleashed the flood, and a moment later Jason was listening to a story that appalled him. He felt sick. He wondered how the woman could have stored such venom without anyone noticing.

Torran was safely tucked up with Jan sitting beside her, waiting for the doctor who appeared to be spending an unconscionable time with the housekeeper.

Lyan, drinking whisky and eating sandwiches, felt as if the day had lasted for a week. Will had gone home, worried about Lucy and also his mother, who he felt had too many problems. They were all shattered by his father's sudden death. There were so many arrangements to make and he didn't know how to deal with his sister. Misery dominated him as he drove back to the farm.

The Colonel's burns proved superficial. The district nurse, who had driven up when she saw the fire, dressed them. He had fallen asleep in his chair, having sought sanctuary in his den. He was not used to having so many people about. The two dogs were lying beside him, never taking their eyes off him as if afraid they'd be left alone again.

Most of the strangers had vanished. Melissa and her team were busy in the kitchen, with breakfast in mind for the men.

Jason Hall came into the room and glanced at the Colonel. Quint rumbled suddenly and the old man opened his eyes.

'I can't make out what's been going on,' he complained. 'What in the world is wrong with Mrs Burton?'

'She's asleep now,' the doctor said. 'I gave her an injection. I need an ambulance. I'm afraid she's had a complete breakdown. I suspect it's been coming on for some time.

I gather from Lucy's brother that she filled the child with stories that drove her to believe Torran was a witch and ought to be burned. Lucy set fire to the shed, but Mrs Burton put the idea into her head.'

'Surely she didn't intend to kill them?'

'As far as I can make out from what she said—she wasn't very coherent—she meant to frighten them away as she wanted to live in the cottage. She hadn't realised how strong the wind was or that the fire would spread. That's what did the rest of the damage to her mind . . . she had burned her own future home.'

'Even if it had been empty I wouldn't have offered it to her,' the Colonel said. 'She could never have afforded the rent.'

'She's our anonymous letter-writer.' Lyan, who had followed Jason into the room, stifled a yawn. 'I caught her putting one of the letters into the Ardans' mailbox this evening . . . and she poisoned Sapphire. It's all inexplicable.'

The doctor took a sandwich from the plate on the table, and accepted the mug of coffee that Lyan poured. The Colonel was wide awake now.

'I gather from Effie Green that she thought, at first, she'd be setting up house with you here in due course. Even Effie thought that highly unlikely, but Mrs Burton evidently has a romantic turn of mind. When she found you had no intention of treating her as anything but a housekeeper, it began to affect her.'

He helped himself to two more sandwiches.

'I missed my evening meal.' He paused to eat. 'Then you bought the dogs, and she hates dogs . . . and then, even worse, you took a lodger and she had two men to look after. When the schoolmaster moved in the village had the notion that you were more than friends, and that disgusted her, though it explained your lack of interest in her. More mysteriously, given that, there were also stories that you were both visiting Torran for highly immoral purposes . . . a thoroughly mixed-up woman.'

'I never even thought . . . I was sorry for her and I needed a housekeeper. I knew her husband well.' Roger, his thick grey hair standing on end like a crest, reminded Lyan of a bewildered heron. 'What happens now?'

'Hospital . . . probably for a long time. She won't be your responsibility. She'd be better right away from here, with no contact again with any of you. Hopefully, she'll recover.'

'Loneliness, old age, and too much imagination,' Melissa said. She had brought in another plate of sandwiches. 'Jason, your wife said you haven't eaten since lunchtime. Get those inside you and I've made fresh coffee. Before you go, I think you ought to look at Torran. She's badly shocked. Jan's sitting with her, but she can't stop crying.'

'This will bring it all back,' the Colonel said. 'Damn the wretched woman. And what do we do about Lucy?'

'I suspect she's been shocked out of her silliness . . . if you can call it that. I don't know what else to call it. She's an impressionable child, and obviously she's seen a sight too much of Mrs Burton.'

'She bribed the children with cakes and home-made sweets. She makes rare fudge,' Melissa said. 'Her cakes are awful, but children don't seem to care. We could never sell them at the WI. I had to pretend afterwards that they'd been sold right away, and get rid of them. People fought over the fudge. That always went well.'

She dropped into a chair and yawned. 'Will's taken my old boy home. If he doesn't get some sleep there'll be no sermon on Sunday. He'll be too exhausted. He is sure to want to use tonight's events and do a major rewrite which will take all tomorrow.'

She yawned again.

'I'm whacked. I wonder what interpretation he'll put

197

on it all. He has a very muddled view of the world at the best of times, and this has thoroughly confused him. He can't believe that people really can be wicked.'

Lyan was so tired that he had begun to lose track of events. He dropped into bed at last, and slept until well after lunch. Shaved and dressed, he went downstairs to find Torran officiating in the kitchen.

'Better?' he asked.

'Much.' She smiled at him. There were still dark circles under her eyes, and she had no colour, but she seemed brighter. 'People have been so kind ... I would never have believed it of them. And the doctor's given me some pills, just for the next few days.'

She was busy cutting bread and putting slices in the big toaster.

'I heard Amber barking. She and Silver and Missie were standing by the cottage. Silver was banging on the front door, which is still there, amazingly. The front room is almost undamaged apart from smoke and water. They're fine.'

She put toast in front of him and then fetched the coffee jug.

'Everyone's been helping feed my invalids. So many people have called. Effie's busy making beds.'

Lyan helped himself to several slices of toast. 'I don't know what meal this is—breakfast or lunch. I'm starving.'

'Tea, I should think,' Torran said. 'I can't get that poor woman out of my mind. If I'd known that she'd been filling the children up with lies ... Will came this morning to see how we were. He feels so bad about Lucy. She'd have helped me with the animals if she'd known about them, he says. The police know it was started deliberately ... everyone's wondering what they'll do about her.'

'Maybe not a lot, as Mrs Burton incited her. Where is everybody?' Lyan asked, spreading butter and home-made marmalade. For all her odd ways, they would miss Dorothy Burton. She had done her job very well.

'Grandfather and the Colonel have gone to look at the cottage and meet the insurance people. The Colonel suggested that we have a flat here instead, as it's going to be some time before it's repaired. Then Jan and I can help with the housekeeping, and in return we get free board and lodging. I hadn't realised how big this is.'

'Nine bedrooms and attics,' Lyan said. 'Room for an army.'

Torran laughed.

'It would be a very small army.'

He led the way to the little den. Torran followed him. She stared at the photograph on the bureau.

'That's my mother! What's it doing here? I've never seen that picture of her before.'

Lyan did not know how to answer. He was so used to the photograph that he had forgotten it. Torran had never been in the den before. He watched as she picked up the album that lay beside it, and began to turn the pages. He knew the contents, which included a wedding photo-graph, as well as pictures of Torran from babyhood on.

'My mother was married to the Colonel ... that *is* the Colonel?' She looked at him with puzzled eyes. 'He can't be my father ... my father's dead ... she wasn't married three times?'

She hadn't noticed the two men standing silent in the doorway. Sapphire ran to her and greeted her, thrusting her nose against her leg.

'Your father thought it better if you believed he was dead,' Jan said, going to her. He took the album and laid it on the table and then took both her hands. 'He worked for Army Intelligence as well as being in the Army ... he could never be a major part of your life and he and your mother thought it would be less of a disruption for you to know nothing about him. You were only six months old when they decided to divorce, as by then your mother had met your stepfather.'

'Then when we came here?'

'I was offering my daughter a home,' Roger Manton said. 'I didn't intend to tell you, ever. I thought it best. It was such a long time ago and I had never shared your life . . . I didn't see how we could make up lost ground.'

Torran picked up the album again, turning the pages, looking at herself as a toddler, in school uniform, riding her horse, cutting a birthday cake . . . a record of her life until they came to England.

'I sent them to him,' Jan said. 'It was the least I could do.'

'I was too old for her,' the Colonel said. 'I was over forty and she was only twenty-one. Younger than you are now and she was far less mature. It was crazy. Steve was only two years older than she. I was away for so long, and often out of touch. I've never forgotten her . . . and never regretted it, except that I lost you both.'

He looked at her anxiously.

'You will stay? It's been wonderful having you close, knowing you were safe, watching over you. I always hoped you'd come and visit.'

'We'll stay,' Torran said. 'I need to get used to the idea . . . I can't take it in. Too much has happened in the past twenty-four hours.' She sat quiet, stroking Sapphire, who was leaning against her knee. Somewhere in the night the terrors that had ridden her for so long had vanished, and the panic had gone. One shock driving out another? She didn't know.

Melissa came into the room, carrying a huge bouquet of flowers and several parcels.

'The flowers are from Lucy's mother. She's devastated,' she said. 'The village seems to be suffering from guilt. They've sent tins of cakes and pies and biscuits. It looks like Christmas downstairs. Effie's in the kitchen too, sure that Torran's too upset to bother with cooking. She's offered to come in daily until you're all on your feet again.'

'We sound like wimps,' the Colonel said, irritated.

Melissa laughed.

'Let them fuss you. They're all feeling bad. Effie's nonsense has come home to roost and she feels responsible as she first told Mrs Burton the old stories about the witch and you know how her imagination can run away with her. What she doesn't know she invents and her inventions are always lurid. Probably because she leads such a dull life herself. She's trying to make amends.'

Torran sat quietly, thankful to have Sapphire beside her to stroke. She had a father who was alive . . . a man who had cared about her all those years although he never saw her. Who had condemned himself to loneliness so that she should not suffer from the difficulties of having two separate families.

It was the second time that her life had been turned upside down, the second time she had lost her home. She stared into the fire that Melissa had lit, thinking it would bring comfort, and wondered what the future might hold.

Eighteen

The villagers of Lynsom Green were shocked back to their senses. Nobody wanted to admit to being part of a plot to evict newcomers, even if they did resent them. They had never dreamt that anyone could go to such lengths.

Alison Cartwright found willing visitors who came to help, offered to cook, to look after the children, to collect eggs, to do any little job that would ease her days.

Everyone understood that her life would be immeasurably improved without Jim, his constant inroads on their income for his drinking, and his violent rages. No one said so. Never speak ill of the dead.

Will, feeling tension drain away from him, was, at times, inclined to wonder at the sudden apparent canonisation that had fallen upon his father, but if that was how people behaved, he was not going to question it. Even the animals seemed to sense that life had fallen into pleasanter grooves. Jim's rages had often led him to hit them as well as his family.

Lucy crept around like a small ghost, but that was preferable to her usual insolence and refusal to do anything she was told. Davey did not call. His father, shocked by the cottage fire, thought the children better apart. George Prentice wondered if it was only luck that his son hadn't been involved. He, too, had much to consider. He had not realised just how impressionable children could be.

Two days after the fire, while quieting Quint's frequent protests at the number of visitors, the Colonel felt as if his home had become public property.

He went out into the scullery, and discovered, to his

surprise, that Effie was already there, competently bottle-feeding a small black scrap that clung desperately to her finger with tiny claws and flexed its hind paws as it drank.

'I had to do this with Cass,' she said. 'Brings it all back. Someone threw him away in a plastic bag. Luckily I kept the bottles. Mac's sent food for the various birds and animals, as everything was destroyed.'

The Colonel looked at her, startled. He had not thought of that. Effie seemed to take it for granted that there would be such help. She went on talking, enjoying her new role.

'I'd like one of these. My boy's getting old, and Mark Luton's mum says he can have a cat, so that's two homes found. Won't be a problem. There's always someone looking for a kitten. If the worst comes to the worst, they'll take them at Cartwrights'. You can never have too many cats on a farm. Or owls. Plagued with rats and mice.'

She took a tissue and dipped it in olive oil, rubbing it gently over the small underparts.

'No mother to stimulate them and help them eliminate, so I have to do it. I wonder if Sapphire would help? If she would just lick them . . .' Anything was worth a try, she thought. 'That would be more natural and less likely to harm the babies.'

Sapphire adored babies, whether they were puppies or kittens, and showed every sign of wanting to mother them. The Colonel brought her in, much to Quint's dismay. He was far too brash and seemed unable to do anything gently, so he was excluded. His mournful complaints continued for several minutes.

Roger transferred the kittens to Sapphire's own bed, which he also brought in. She settled to wash each of the tiny creatures, and they, delighted to have a warm body to cuddle against, accepted her at once. Within minutes she and Effie were a team.

203

The second kitten was vociferous, demanding its bottle. In spite of its blindness it reacted to the scent of milk on her fingers, trying to suck them.

'It's amazing how much noise such a tiny creature can make.' There was an odd rusty sound, which the Colonel identified as an unpractised purr emanating from the kitten that had just been fed, responding to Sapphire's warmth and comforting tongue, though it did seem to make the little animal look as if someone had tried to drown him.

Roger had never liked Effie, aware of her scandal-inventing tongue, but he was impressed.

'I can come up and help every day,' she said. 'My life's full of empty hours. Be glad of something useful to do. Can stay as long as you want.' He suddenly realised she was afraid he would reject her or think she was imposing herself upon them.

'We'd be grateful,' he said. 'There's too much for Torran to do here. Jan is handy round the house. I'm ashamed to say that Lyan and I are useless. Mrs Burton never let us do anything and we've been spoiled. The Army doesn't give you much scope for cooking and cleaning.'

Lyan, who had looked after himself for some years after his divorce, would not have been flattered to hear he too was considered incapable.

'If you can coppice woodland you can clean out cages.' Effie was now feeding the third kit. 'I didn't know she had so many beasts.'

The Colonel was amazed at the amount of work. There were water bowls to fill and hungry animals demanding nourishment. Jan prepared the feeds, knowing what each needed. It was one of his daily chores. Many of the little animals demanded affection, wanting stroking and cuddling. They were all extremely tame.

Torran spent a great deal of her time dressing injuries. Effie so enjoyed feeding the kittens that she left that chore to her, with Sapphire helping busily, enchanted by her new role.

The knowledge that Roger was her father, coming on top of the fire, had silenced Torran completely, so that she sat, in the evening, staring into the flames, remote from all of them, worrying both the older men immensely. Neither realised that she had no idea how to treat him, and was bewildered by his new position in her life.

'She needs time,' Lyan said. 'Time to know you; time to understand the past and why it happened as it did; time perhaps to forgive her mother for what she feels was her deceit; and Steve and Jan too. Coming on top of the fire she must feel as if her whole world has fallen apart and everything she thought she knew about it has been changed.'

Ours too, the Colonel thought, with his home invaded not only by extra people but by birds and animals. He had not realised that he and Lyan had a settled routine. Effie cooked for all of them, and cleaned up as well. The dogs, after an initial wariness, soon realised that she enjoyed their company and that the kitchen was no longer forbidden territory.

Melissa called in one morning, bringing a case full of spare clothes. The back seat of the car was piled high with parcels.

'People've sent bedding and kitchen utensils . . . all kinds of things,' she said. 'They can't do enough. I suppose the cottage will be rebuilt?'

'I hope so. It's a shame, as it was listed and very attractive. It won't look the same; we can't replace age. I only hope they don't condemn it out of hand and say nothing can be built there again.'

'Is that likely?' Melissa asked.

'I've no idea. There are so many rules and regulations these days.'

He sighed, and took up his pipe. He put it down, and

then picked it up again and filled it. Effie, who had brought in a tray of mugs filled with coffee, smiled at him in approval.

'I like to see a man with a pipe. Gives him an air of authority and makes me feel he's competent. My father was a pipe-smoker.'

Melissa, refusing to stay at first, changed her mind, but perched on the window seat like a bird about to fly.

'Makes me feel criminal.' Roger sucked deeply then took his own mug and dropped into one of the armchairs. 'There's so much written against it. Mrs Burton behaved as if I had committed every sin in the calendar if I dared to smoke. I rarely have more than two pipes a week. I doubt if that's going to kill me.' He picked up his mug. 'She came into the room, sniffed, then flung all the windows wide and walked around like an avenging angel.'

'Whatever else she was, she was never an angel,' Lyan said, coming into the room at that juncture. He glanced down the track to the ruined cottage, which seemed to be surrounded by people. Tarpaulins covered the ruined roof, but nothing else had been done. 'There's nothing there to loot, is there?'

'Nothing.' The Colonel stood up. 'Better see what's going on.'

Melissa, following them, went to her car and drove off, waving, while the two men walked through the smoke-darkened trees.

Half the village appeared to have congregated in front of the ruined buildings. Davey Prentice was watching from a distance as his father was among the little crowd. The councillor turned as Roger approached.

'We were wondering if anything could be salvaged,' he said. 'Everyone's upset. Jack here can mend anything made of wood or metal, and make it look as good as new. He thought we might find a few things and he could save them having to be replaced. Expensive business these days.'

'Not a lot left,' Jack Grindle said. He specialised in repairs since he had been laid off as a result of a takeover of the small furniture manufacturers for which he had worked in Pyneton. 'A few pictures from upstairs, only stained by smoke. One bedroom was more or less untouched and the furniture seems to have survived; probably only needs a clean-up. The bedding's undamaged but it stinks. There's nothing left in the downstairs rooms. Part of the house is left, but it will all have to come down.' He was a small man, grey-haired, with intensely vivid blue eyes.

'We can all help save some of the rebuilding costs.' George Prentice looked anxious, as if afraid their offers might be rejected. 'There are plasterers, decorators, tilers . . . all do it for a very small fee or for nothing, depending on how much business they have. Long evenings coming, and weekends; be up again in no time. Also some of the men who are out of work will be glad of worthwhile occupation.'

'People never cease to amaze me,' the Colonel said, as they re-entered the Place. The vet's Land-Rover was parked in the drive.

'They're in the sanctuary.' Effie paused on her way with yet another tray. Lyan, after some thought, deduced that she meant the scullery, where all the cages had been put. He led the way.

Torran, oddly dressed in Melissa's trousers, which were slightly too long and had to be turned up, and a jersey that was too short in the arms, was bending over a large collapsible cage that Lyan had not seen before. Inside it, as far away from the onlookers as possible, were Ric and his foster-mother. She hissed at them, but was so weak that it was only a gesture.

The vet had brought them back that morning.

'Try to have as little to do with them as possible,' Mac said. 'I think they should be released. There are hardly any foxes left on the hill but Ric may find a mate. It's doubtful if the cat will domesticate. She's used to freedom.'

The young fox was cuddled close against her. He watched the onlookers, but the cat was tense, every muscle taut, her eyes staring at them with an unwavering amber gaze.

She hurt all over, as the bites were deep. Ric, also in pain, was young enough to adapt to new surroundings. Torran looked at him, yearning to pick him up and comfort him, to tame him and keep him, but knew it would be wrong. She draped an old curtain over the side of the cage to give them privacy.

Alison Cartwright was waiting in the den, Lucy, white-faced, beside her.

'She wants to apologise,' she said. 'It won't be much help, but it will be something.'

Lucy stared up as if terrified that she might be hit. The men watched from the other side of the room. Torran, with sudden vivid memories of her own panic attacks, walked over to the child and took her in her arms.

'You don't really think I'm a witch, do you?' she asked.

Lucy shook her head.

'Will says you like animals. I need help with mine. Would you like to come and help feed and clean cages, and wash the bowls and give them water? I can show you how to look after them when they're hurt and then you can help your mother and Will on the farm.' She stood up and took Lucy's hand. 'Come and peep at the cub and the cat; they were hurt by the terriers, but they're going to be all right.'

'She's only a baby,' her mother said defensively, when they had left the room. 'Too young to work out what's true and untrue when it's adults telling her. What will they do to her?'

'Not a lot, I suspect,' Lyan said. 'She's obviously appalled by what she's done and that's punishment enough. She'll probably get away with a good lecture. If she promises to behave, and keeps her word, I'll vouch for her. None of us realised what was going on. I'd no idea the children even knew Mrs Burton.'

'Lucy told Will she made them sweets and told them stories; not good stories, but who's to know? Some of the old ones are bad enough. Bluebeard and tales of witches eating little children . . . Enough to give them nightmares.'

She looked up at Lyan with pleading eyes.

'Our Lucy always did believe what she was told. The last to stop believing in Santa and the tooth fairy, and sure that there are ghosts and witches. She's an odd child . . . we knew most of what she said was imagination and non-sense; maybe we didn't really listen to her, and could have stopped what was going on.'

Torran was startled by the gifts they received and the kindness of the villagers. She had expected to feel the familiar panic, sleeping in a strange room and plunged suddenly among so many people. Instead, she felt as if she had been given a new freedom.

'They'll build you a proper hospital,' Effie said. 'You'll need it. Now they know what you do, you'll find a lot more birds and little animals will come to you. Mostly people either take them to Mac, who may put them to sleep, or try to heal them themselves, and then they die.'

Effie found immense satisfaction in her new role, a purpose in life, and a sense of humour no one had realised she possessed. She no longer had a need to invent strange stories: there was enough happening all the time. Within a few days Torran had added another tiny deer to her ménage, its mother having died when it was born. Lyan heard it bleating one night when he went out to film and Effie, bottle-feeding it, was enchanted.

Life changed for all of them, and both Lyan and the Colonel hoped that the cottage would take a long time to rebuild. The old house was alive as it had never been before and the dogs were rejuvenated, delighted to have so many people to fuss them.

Mark collected his new kitten and Effie took hers home, only to find that Cass resented it bitterly and refused to make friends. They had to be kept in separate rooms while she was out, as she now worked at Staghill Place from nine to five.

Filming became a major part of Lyan's life, with Torran as his constant companion, both of them absorbed in the wildlife on the hill. Missie and Silver, once all the excitement had died away, always came to meet them. Both were baffled by the lack of a front door on which to rap, as the cottage had now been razed to the ground and new building begun.

Silver showed an unexpected jealousy, always positioning himself between Lyan and Torran and butting Torran away if he came too near, an action that amused both of them.

'I suspect he thinks you're a doe and part of his harem,' Lyan said.

'Or his mother.' The past was fading, the present more rewarding than Torran had expected.

The deer never ventured into the garden at the Place, though they were curious about the newcomer who followed Effie and Torran like a little dog. Lucy, allowed to bottle-feed, fell in love, and adored the new fawn.

Time passed quickly. Ric, released, was hunting on the hill, while the cat, whom they named Mitzi, came back to rear her new litter in safety, accepting that here was a security she had never known before. The kittens were born in a small barn, at the other side of the big yard behind the Colonel's house. She hid them in a hole in the rafters and everyone wondered how they would ever come down, but she solved that problem when they were four weeks old by carrying each one in her mouth, and nesting in the hay.

Although she would have nothing to do with people, she allowed the kittens to be cuddled and played with. When they were six weeks old she deserted them, leaving them to Torran's care.

'I ought to have her spayed,' Torran said, 'but it would mean trapping her and would be a horrible experience for her. If she continues to have kittens here we can tame them and find homes for them; she's far too wild to have much to do with us.'

Lyan filmed Ric with his foster-mother. They had formed a strong attachment and were to be seen basking in the sunshine, the cat lying beside the fox, occasionally washing him as if he were another cat. Everyone was sure that it would be a most unusual documentary.

Excitement returned to Staghill.

Nineteen

One night in June, a year after the fire, Lyan was sitting on a rock at the top of Staghill. There was a Hunter's Moon, an enormous glowing orb, high in a starlit sky. He hoped that Torran would join him. It was the Colonel's birthday and she had made him a cake and felt she ought to spend part of her evening with her father. Though they were on friendly terms, she could not yet bring herself to hug or kiss him, feeling he was still a stranger.

Time to take stock, Lyan felt, hoping that the woods would soon come to life. Below him the village lay, almost a different place. Eileen Carton had decided to retire early, but called regularly, helping with the many birds and small animals that Torran had thrust upon her.

He was headmaster now, with a new young assistant, a little bewildered and trying to find her own place in the community. With so many people about him all the time, he seemed never to have space in which to think.

Effie was not the only one who had been affected by the events of the past year. Mark, now at the senior school, was a frequent visitor as were his mother and her husband when he was home. Mark had his own foal; he had his own cat. Breen was now a large animal with green eyes, and too much skill in catching small birds. The boy chattered to his mother as he never had before.

Lucy, shocked into sudden adulthood, planned to be an animal nurse and spent her free time with Torran, helping with the wildlife hospital which was now well known. George Prentice, unexpectedly interested, had helped turn the little sanctuary into a charity. He had run a bazaar and pet show to raise money, bringing in an amazing sum of over six hundred pounds. The men helping with the cottage had built a large breeze-block barn for the animals.

The Cartwright farm was thriving.

Lyan's thoughts roamed, carefully avoiding the real issue: Torran. She too had changed, was almost, Jan said, as she had been before they left Africa, but she was still wary of strange men.

She talked to him of her hopes, of the animals that came into the hospital, and accepted his help with them. She treated him like a favourite brother, but that was not what he wanted.

He was afraid to tempt fate, to force a final rejection. Although he thought he detected signs that she was beginning to relax with all of them and there were moments when she forgot her fears and laughed joyously, it was, he realised, only when animals were present. They seemed to give her a confidence that was lacking when she was with people, and no dog or cat around. Only Jan was trusted enough to hug her when she needed comfort. She hugged the dogs and she hugged Silver and Missie. When she was tired she preferred their company.

Lyan heard her footsteps on the hill. He wanted to reach out to her, to draw her down to sit beside him, to put an arm round her. She leaned against the rocky outcrop, close enough to touch, but he dared not. Somewhere below them Ric and his mate had cubs.

'Have you seen them tonight?' she asked softly.

'Not yet.'

The full moon slipped up the sky. Small white clouds passed across its face.

'It looks as if the moon's running,' Torran said, watching the wisps blow fast across the golden ball. A small wind rustled fallen leaves that smelled of recent rain.

A head appeared in the bushes and Lyan drew in his

breath as Ric nosed Torran. In spite of her care not to bond, he came to her for food when it was scarce. He looked at her, one paw raised, almost as if questioning this human who had healed him when he was hurt, and who shared the feeding of his mate and his cubs.

Above him stood Mitzi, looking down, but never coming near, never asking for a caressing hand, although she too knew there would be food when the winter bit hard, and that there was always a safe place to rear her kittens.

Below them, in the little clearing, the four cubs ventured cautiously from the den, small heads curious, looking up at their father and the cat. The vixen, who had never known contact with people, was wild and wary. She was afraid, but needed to be near her babies, every instinct driving her to protect them.

She watched the two humans, used to their presence, but ready to gather the cubs and run if they moved.

Ric had brought her a young rabbit that Will had shot. He did not share his father's prejudices about foxes and badgers and was as intrigued by the wildlife on the hill as Lyan and Torran, occasionally joining Lyan on a nighttime filming session.

The cat, apparently deciding that she also had a share in Ric's family, brought mice daily. That too Lyan had been able to record.

Watching them as she stood behind Lyan, Torran was worried. They had interfered with nature, making Ric trust them; the cubs were playful and had learnt that these people did not mean danger. Would they react in the same way to others? Had they any right to meddle? Yet if they had not rescued Mitzi and Ric, both would most probably have died.

Lyan, filming, was absorbed.

Torran's work with the animals was unhindered. People now brought not only wild creatures found injured, birds rescued from cats or fallen from the nest when only half-fledged, but also orphan puppies and kittens, and, dis-mayingly, small animals like hamsters, rabbits and gerbils that children no longer wanted. No one seemed to realise that each new mouth meant more need for food, and both and she Jan were working with their carvings and paintings in every spare moment to make enough money to keep them all.

Effie, becoming protective, accepted the newcomers and asked for donations towards their keep, as no one else would do so. Watching the cubs, Torran's thoughts roamed anxiously. Suppose they were orphaned too? She was always afraid that the foxes would become the target of terriers again. Their peace was fragile.

The vixen, her worry flaring when a sudden gust of wind teased the trees, chivvied her little family to safety. Ric and the cat vanished. Lyan thought he heard footsteps on the rock and looked around him, but saw nothing. There had been no intruders on the hill since the night, a year ago, when three men had killed a deer. Nobody could now come unseen. Or could they? He felt uneasy.

Suddenly there was a gleaming shape as Silver came to greet them, his hooves tapping on the hard surface. Missie slipped out of the shadows, as pleased as the white stag to see them both. They were far too tame, Torran thought, and voiced her worry.

'Silver's an outcast anyway,' Lyan said. 'Missie has attached to him. Their instincts have been changed. They live as if we were part of their herd, coming to us for food and trusting us completely, but only when we're on our own.'

They began the walk home, the two deer following. The church clock struck two. Tomorrow was Saturday and the Ardans were moving. They intended to celebrate in the evening at the Dog and Duck, the village taking an immense pride in the completion. He would miss them terribly, even though they would still be near. He would miss the meals together, the knowledge that they were all under the same roof. Like him, they had their own quarters.

There was a bleat from the heather. A tiny fawn, cuddled against the ground, gazed up at Torran with wondering brown eyes.

'Lyan, look!'

He gave a sigh of pleasure. The little animal was pure white.

'It must be Silver's. Missie hasn't had her baby yet.'

There was a hind hiding in the bushes. She came anxiously towards them and stamped her hoof. They left the little one and went on down the hill. Lyan put his arm, without thinking, around Torran's shoulders. She relaxed against him and they walked on together, the two deer following. He felt a sudden exultation, but said nothing.

One day, he thought. One day we'll live in the cottage, and Jan and the Colonel will spend their old age enjoying one another's company. I'll be Roger's son-in-law, he realised suddenly and found the idea pleased him.

The house was quiet when they reached home, the windows dark. Quint was silent, knowing their footsteps, and the sound of the key in the door. Sapphire left guarding to him, only joining in if she felt there was real danger.

Torran went quietly upstairs, pausing for a moment to put a hand to Lyan's face, and smile up at him. The fear that had enveloped her had vanished and life was normal again.

There might be insecurity in the world outside, but here she was cherished. She realised quite suddenly how much consideration the Colonel had shown in deciding not to be part of her life when she was a baby. A flood of affection for him both startled and overwhelmed her.

She smiled at him as he came out of his bedroom, tying

the girdle round the dressing-gown that gave him the look of an austere monk. An appearance, Torran now knew, that was entirely deceptive: she had watched him relaxing with the dogs. She was excited by her news.

'There's a new fawn on the hill,' she said. 'He's white, like his father. Another to add to the legend.' She looked at him, concerned, as he did not answer her. His face was grey and his mouth tight with pain. 'Can't you sleep?'

'This damned arthritis. It comes out of the blue. I was looking for pain-killers.'

'Go back to bed. I'll find them and bring you a hot drink. One of Jan's special herbal brews. It tastes pleasant and will help you sleep.'

The Colonel watched her run down the stairs again, envying her youth and mobility. Painfully, he went back into his room and eased himself into bed. Sapphire came across the floor, always anxious about her master, and sat beside him, her head against his hand, aware of his discomfort. Quint was in his own bed, too lazy to move. He rolled on his back and beat his tail against the wall. The Colonel, in spite of his pain, laughed at the dog.

Torran, busy in the kitchen, suddenly realised that the frightening memories were fading, pushed into the background as she allowed people into her life and accepted their willing help. She worked deftly, adding honey to sweeten the brew. The Colonel had been searching, she knew, for conventional pain-killers. They were kept in the big bathroom, but after a moment's thought she substituted one of Jan's homoeopathic remedies.

She sat on the chair by her father's bed and watched him drink. He had expected bitterness, but it tasted sweet. He revelled in the knowledge that this was his daughter, and she was caring for him.

Torran suddenly felt comfortable with him. He was as much in need of her care as her animal patients. She longed to ease his pain.

'It'll do you good,' she said. 'Jan swears by it and by the pills. He's a chronic sufferer. What do you do to yourselves to get arthritis?'

'That's a bit like asking, "Why is the moon?" ' the Colonel said, easing himself against the pillows that Torran had heaped behind his back. It was years since any woman had thought of his comfort.

The silly phrase brought back a memory of Nerine, who had a habit of asking unaswerable questions. 'Why is a fish a fish?' she had asked one day. She was seven years old. Torran found herself mystified by the question.

'Why is a fish a fish?' she had repeated, puzzled.

'Yes.'

The child was impatient with her, knowing very well what she was trying to say and feeling that her big sister was too stupid to answer. 'Why isn't a fish a dog and a dog a cat and the moon the sun?'

'Penny for them,' The Colonel said, wondering at her silence. She seemed to have forgotten him. Sapphire thrust her nose against Torran's knee.

She laughed at the memory, discovering as she did so that she could think of her half-sisters without pain.

The Colonel listened and then smiled.

'She was puzzled by words. Why do they call a fish a fish, instead of calling it a dog? What makes each word specific so that we all understand one another? Is that what she meant?'

'You're the first person to realise that,' Torran said. 'Nerine was so funny; she asked the most astonishing questions. Like "Why is God?" and "Where does night go when day comes?" '

She sighed.

'I do miss them. They were much younger than me, but we had so much fun together. Lysbeth was even crazier about horses than I was, but for her other animals didn't exist.'

'Your mother was afraid of dogs when I knew her. Did she get over that?'

'She was younger then than I am now.' It was an astonishing thought, as was the idea of her mother being married to the Colonel. 'We had dogs. She seemed old to me; old and wise. She was very comforting if we were ill or hurt ourselves. She was very kind to everybody, and if one of the African children on the farm was ill, she helped to nurse him. That's why it was so cruel . . . she never harmed anyone . . .'

The tears that came were unexpected. The Colonel put his arms round her and held her until they stopped. He wiped his own eyes surreptitiously, memory reminding him of a girl who had laughed with him and loved every moment of her life until he went away.

Torran sat up and dried her eyes and sniffed.

'I'm sorry . . . I don't allow myself to remember as a rule.'

'Better to remember. They'll always be a part of your life. I wish I'd known your sisters.' I wish you'd grown up with me, he thought. I missed so much.

She looked down at him as she picked up the glass, and was about to say goodnight.

She put it back on the bedside table and hugged him again. He held her as if he would never let go. After all these lonely years, he had a daughter to comfort him. The thought followed him into his dreams.

Torran closed the door behind her. For the first time, she felt that she now had a father. A new life stretched ahead of her and she was involved with animals for ever. She looked out of the landing window at the darkened woods and thought of the deer hiding there. There was a movement in the shadows and a flash of silver and she knew that the deer was nearby, perhaps waiting for her, but she was too tired to go out again.

Hope, that had long been a stranger, returned and

stayed with her as she slept, so that her dreams were no longer nightmares, but of the new fawns that played in the woods and followed their father.

Lyan sat by the window in his room, looking out, also thinking of the future. There was time, all the time in the world, and he was confident that his ambitions would be fulfilled. The films were now a reality, due to be released next year. More were wanted.

The children loved the pictures of Torran with the animals. He had shown those in school. Several had met the deer, Torran showing them how to crouch quietly, while Silver and Missie fed. They knew better now than to run and chase any animals.

Lyan often asked her to bring any new patients that were well enough to come into the classroom, and Torran's hospital became part of the school lore, featuring in many essays. Even Davey Prentice had taken one of Mitzi's kittens which, brought up by humans from six weeks old, soon became tame.

He had learnt a sharp lesson from the fire-raising incident. He was doing well at his new school and, much to everyone's surprise, helped Will on the farm and enjoyed working with the cattle.

Lyan was lost in his reveries. He had plans for an educational film, showing children how to approach animals, how to feed them, how to care for their own small companions. Amber now accepted people and was as much at ease as any dog. She would have a role to play, emphasising her history and how Torran had helped her overcome her fear. She was an important part of the household.

She slept in Torran's room but by day she was as likely to shadow Quint as to join Silver and Missie, if her mistress were not near.

Sequences came into his head. His concept was brilliant. It was original. Nobody had ever produced anything like it. Excitement prevented him from sleeping. He went to his desk, and spent hours making notes, his mind spinning, full of ideas.

Later, standing at the window, watching the sun blaze on the horizon, flooding the world with colour again, he thought of the deer. There had always been tales about Staghill, but they changed with each generation.

He was struck with an idea for yet another film, starting his own legend, about a healer who gave her time to the animals, keeping them safe from intruders. About the white stags that brought good fortune and kept the village safe.

Just as Gibraltar needed its apes, and the Tower of London needed the ravens, so Lynsom Green needed Silver and his progeny. It was a story to captivate the children.

The tiny white fawn lying in the heather was a symbol of good fortune and not of disaster. The white deer, throughout the centuries, were the true Guardians of Staghill.